CONFRONTATIONS

CONFRONTATIONS

A Novel

SIMONE ATANGANA BEKONO

TRANSLATED BY SUZANNE HEUKENSFELDT JANSEN

BLOOMSBURY PUBLISHING
NEW YORK · LONDON · OXFORD · NEW DELHI · SYDNEY

BLOOMSBURY PUBLISHING
Bloomsbury Publishing Inc.
1385 Broadway, New York, NY 10018, USA

BLOOMSBURY, BLOOMSBURY PUBLISHING, and the Diana logo are trademarks of
Bloomsbury Publishing Plc

First published in Dutch by Lebowski, 2020, Netherlands
First published in Great Britain in 2023 by Serpent's Tail, an imprint of Profile Books Ltd
First published in the United States by Bloomsbury Publishing 2024

Copyright © Simone Atangana Bekono, 2020
Translation copyright © Suzanne Heukensfeldt Jansen, 2023

This publication has been made possible with financial support from the
Dutch Foundation for Literature.

ISBN: HB: 978-1-63973-091-9; EBOOK: 978-1-63973-092-6

Library of Congress Cataloging-in-Publication Data is available.

2 4 6 8 10 9 7 5 3 1

Typeset in Freight Text by MacGuru Ltd
Designed by Barneby Ltd
Printed and bound in the U.S.A.

To find out more about our authors and books visit www.bloomsbury.com and
sign up for our newsletters.

Bloomsbury books may be purchased for business or promotional use. For information on
bulk purchases please contact Macmillan Corporate and Premium Sales Department at
specialmarkets@macmillan.com.

CONFRONTATIONS

I REMEMBER HOW WE ALL stood in front of the gate. It was the end of the year for Year 6 or 7. We'd had PE outside on the small green in between the gym and the asylum seekers' centre and were on our way back to school. The teacher was a bit further ahead with the other children, but one of us stopped to look at the man, and so the rest of the group came to a halt as well. The man was tall and thin and was wearing a threadbare winter coat that hung around him like a cloud. His slender, black face seemed to disappear into the upturned collar. He was standing next to the barriers, in the grass.

Someone threw the first coin, I think it was Sjoerd, and more boys than girls joined in. Holding my gym bag in my hand, I stood there looking at my classmates, how they rummaged in the pockets of their trousers and denim jackets.

'Why are you doing that?' Liliana asked Teun.

'He needs money, doesn't he?' He laughed. No one had more than a few coins on them. It was soon over.

The man was staring at us from behind the gate, as the coins lay glistening in front of his feet. I didn't want him to pick them up. I remember thinking that was extremely important, that he didn't pick them up.

'Pick them up! Pick them up!' Sjoerd and Teun, as well as the other boys and a few of the girls shouted. They laughed at the man. The teacher turned around. She called out that we had to follow the rest of the class. Everyone ran towards her, laughing. This included Liliana, after she beckoned me.

'Come on!' she called, but I didn't come.

I looked at the man. He looked at me. Neither of us looked at the euro coins in the grass. Then the man turned around, first his head, then his body. He walked back to the asylum seekers' centre.

THE PHOTO IS TAKEN in a small room with grey walls. On one of them, a poster of a spotty boy, photographed face-on and in profile. I have to go and stand against another wall and, as I'm looking at the spotty boy, notice that it's an instruction poster: this is how you take an ID picture of a juvenile delinquent. Face-on and in profile. After the camera's clicked I turn to the left, letting the flashlight brush my right cheek.

The man shuffles to a desk in the corner of the room and downloads the photo onto a computer screen. A tired, sad face looks at him. Is that me? I want to ask, because I'm not sure. He says something about what will happen to my details.

'We might take a further set of fingerprints when you leave, for comparison.'

'For comparison?' I ask.

'Hardly ever happens.'

I once saw a film in which two bank robbers scorched their fingerprints. Fingers bleeding, they set fire to their identity papers, and cut up their passports. The bank robbers were played by two good-looking American actors with unscarred faces. I'm not a good-looking American actor. I'm myself and I'm scarred. One scar, next to my nose, is old and brown from the time that Miriam accidentally burned me with the hair straightener. The other one's new, a pink crescent running from my bottom lip to my chin.

'Do you give us permission to search your body for prohibited articles before you enter the institution?' the man asks. I rub the black ink on the tips of my index fingers against the black on the tips of my thumbs, but it's not coming off.

'Yes.'

The man leaves the room, and I'm alone for a moment, long enough to start sobbing, but then a woman enters.

'I'm going to search you briefly,' she says. 'Follow me.'

We walk over to a new space, almost like a bathroom, but one you might see in a horror film; the grouting between the wall tiles is black with mould, a sucking noise gurgles from behind a low wall. Bad vibes, Liliana would say. It smells of latex and rot here.

First she checks my trousers, shirt, jumper and then my hair. Every now and then she pulls the tangles in my Afro and says sorry. I have to get undressed. I place my clothes on a folding chair with a tear in the backrest's leather. Foam stuffing is trying to worm its way out.

She can look in all my orifices. Bent over forwards, backwards, arms high or low. I can also do the splits, I want to say, but there's no need for that. It's not me anyway. My ID has been impounded. I have a pink crescent on my chin that isn't on my passport photo. An iron can burn away a part of who you are, can make it disappear. A scar does something completely different. Who can say if it's really me? Maybe there's a second me who's cycling to school just now, without ink or scars, instead of doing this here. It's 25 February 2008, and there are two Salomés, and I'm just one of them, and maybe not even the original version. When I was finally sentenced and transferred here, Miriam said: 'This ain't exactly *The Cosby Show*, bitch.'

Maybe the Salomé who hasn't got herself up shit creek's doing all the things I can't do now: smoke weed, watch an English film without subtitles, have sex, travel abroad on a plane alone, make a cocktail with a shaker, buy something that costs more than 200 euros in a smart department store, put together a piece of IKEA furniture all by herself. All without a scar on her chin. Unblemished.

The woman returns.

'We're going to test your urine now,' she says.

'Okay,' I respond. She gives me the kit I need for this and leads me to a corner in the bathroom behind the low wall, where a chrome toilet turns out to be the thing producing the sucking noise. There's a support rail next to the toilet for pulling yourself up.

'When you're ready,' says the woman, and she turns her face to the door.

ON THE WAY HERE, I kept thinking about the time I stole Dad's watch. In the living room of our old house there was a low cabinet and one of its drawers was forbidden territory: it's where he kept all his watches and other things Miriam and I weren't allowed to touch. When I was playing on my own, I'd take all the shiny things I could find and drape them all over me; Mum's necklaces, rings she'd inherited from Grandma, scarves with glitter, napkin rings, gold ribbons, even key rings. I felt like a queen. I tied the sleeves of my bathrobe around my neck in a knot like a cape and grabbed the mop from the cleaning cupboard. Then, holding the mop in my hand, I'd walk slowly through my bedroom or along the landing. Once, when Dad was out, I took the watch from his drawer. After I'd finished playing, I forgot to put it back because I'd lost myself in another fantasy game. Only days later did Dad find out that he'd lost his watch. Turned out to be real silver. And engraved in it was a message from his dead mother. A wedding present she'd sent from Cameroon. Dad married Mum in the village church without his family there. They had no money to travel to the Netherlands, but Grandma sent the watch as a wedding present. Two years later, she died. And I'd misplaced that present, he knew it was me straightaway, of course. He roared that I was a magpie and wouldn't be allowed to eat dinner at the table until I'd found it. I looked everywhere, but had no idea where I'd put it. Miriam didn't help, she darted off through the back door and went to play on the little square with other children from the area. Mum couldn't help me, even if she'd wanted to. It took an entire weekend until I finally found it between my mattress and the bed frame. An entire weekend of crying, begging, being ignored, eating in my room, turning drawers upside down, pulling wardrobes away from the wall to look behind them. I hated myself

4

so much that, when I found the watch, I didn't even want to give it back to Dad myself. I gave it to Mum, who gave it to Dad, who put it back in the drawer.

It goes without saying that I learned nothing from this, and not long after, I stole the watch again to play with, but this time I was unceremoniously caught in the act. Dad suddenly appeared in the door frame and I dropped the mop I was prancing back and forth with. The watch sparkled on my wrist. It took Dad less than two steps to reach me, and he hit me so hard in the face that the smack echoed. Mum came running upstairs, because she'd heard the noise I think. I'd fallen to the floor and all three of us, shocked, remained silent. Dad was looking open-mouthed at me, and Mum open-mouthed at Dad. I'm reminded of this incident because, when they shoved me into the police car, he looked in exactly the same way at me. Open-mouthed. Mum came to my rescue that time with the watch, broke the silence by pressing me against her chest and screaming that Dad was crazy for daring to beat his children. He said sorry very quietly, and I found this so sad that, more than anything, I wanted to comfort him. It took another whole day for the awkward mood between us to lift.

What I mean to say is that, on the way here, I also wanted to comfort Dad. Because he was so patently ashamed about the police car, and later in court when I was sentenced, and probably now as well. Because we've hardly talked about what happened. The day things began to unravel, and later the following day when they took me to the police station, is one big, blazing reason to die of shame. Which is what I think he's doing. But, from here, there's nothing I can do to change that.

WHEN I'M READY, THE WOMAN gives me a laminated pass with a lanyard. Then the man who took my photo and couldn't pronounce my name when he checked my details arrives and together they lead me out of the room, into a corridor. The corridor has a curve in it. Or rather, the entire corridor curves. We take a right and continue to go right, past door after door, across lino floors with black sole marks, until we get to a large metal door. The man swipes his pass through a reader next to the door handle; a peep sounds and then a click. The door leads to a small, dark passageway that leads to another large, heavy door. And again that pass: peep, click. Again we take an interminable right turn. I hear the door close behind us like a portcullis, which, *bang*, rams its bars into the earth. They aren't holding on to me, they just walk behind me because they know I can't escape.

'Here,' the woman says. We stop at one of the many blue doors in the corridor. On the door it says 'FRITS VAN GESTEL'. I feel dizzy. The other Salomé may be eating an ice cream with a millionaire in the cafeteria next to school. It's actually too cold for that, but they're doing it anyway, fuck it.

The man knocks on the door, and the man who's called Frits van Gestel opens it. He turns out not to be some random Frits van Gestel, but the person who said that he'd always had respect for 'primitive life here in Africa'. Great respect, he said on TV at the time.

I'm going crazy, I'm thinking. I'd already gone crazy, crazy and wild, but now I'm really spinning out of control. Someone bursts out laughing and I can well understand that, that she has to laugh in a situation like this, because it can't be right. The person who's laughing, laughs abruptly and awkwardly. The man and the woman take a step forward to look at my face, and I gaze left and then right to share my disbelief with them.

6

'What's there to laugh about?' Frits van Gestel asks. He has a deep voice, with a Breda accent. He drops his extended hand.

'Are you all right?' asks the woman. I try to stop my grin by taking my hand to my mouth and pulling it down at the corners, but my jaws aren't playing ball. I nearly have another fit of laughter, I can feel it in my stomach, but, really, I shouldn't.

'Sorry,' I say, and I also take the other hand to my face to cover that laugh with both hands, push it back into my stomach if necessary. 'I'm a bit nervous, I think.'

'Why don't you come and have a seat first,' says Frits van Gestel, as he takes one step to the side so that I can enter his office. 'Then we'll have a look at your file.'

I don't move.

'Is this serious?' I ask, and look at the man and then at the woman again.

'I'm afraid it is,' says the man.

MY NEW ROOM SMELLS LIKE A GYM. That's because of the lino. It's bare, apart from the bag with my things lying on the floor by the little desk underneath the window. A chair's resting with its back against the table top. There's a built-in, open wardrobe to the left of the window. The bed I'm sitting on has a bedside table with a lamp and is pushed against the wall, its head on the side of that vague crap-construction of a WC unit that my previous room also had: a toilet attached to a washbasin with a drawer next to the door. A kind of chrome block. Underneath the basin, next to the drawer, is a hole with a loo roll hanging in it. It's what's considered functional. Two folded towels lie on a small shelf fixed to the wall. Above that shelf hangs a small mirror. On remand I had my own shower.

My room looks out onto grass and railings, and I give my bag, which they've been so decent as to put inside my room, another glance. This is very strange, I think. They usually only take things up to your room in hotels, and this really isn't a hotel.

I move over to my bag, and open it. Inside, my things are packed fairly neatly. I kick the bag towards the open wardrobe and sit down on the bed. All the walls are white here. When, sitting on the bed, I look ahead of me, all I see is a white, empty wall. Apart from some smudges and dirty stains, white. Dark blue curtains hang on either side of the window.

I have to wait for the male and female supervisors, who're coming to collect me when the director, the male and female supervisors themselves and Frits are ready to discuss with me 'what it is that we're going to do here'. This is what Frits van Gestel said, the man from the TV, my behavioural therapist, my mentor. The man with 'great respect for primitive life here in Africa'. I get up again, go to the window, reach over the desk to the curtains and pull them shut.

MY FIRST DAY AT ST ODULF GRAMMAR SCHOOL went like this: I'd cycled there from the village with two boys from primary school who also had scored a test result of 550; precisely the two with whom I'd never really played or talked. The mother of one of them, Joop, had phoned Mum and suggested that, since we were all going to school in town, we might as well cycle there together.

When we arrived at the school's playground, Joop and the other boy, Rens, turned out to have friends in the class already because of some kind of chess tournament. As soon as we'd locked our bikes they were gone. The first period I sat at the back of the classroom with my denim jacket wrapped tightly around me against the draught that blew in through the windows. My form tutor made a fool of himself when he pronounced my name. Kids laughed.

During the lunch break my new classmates and I were taken by a goth from Year 12 to the sports fields next to the playground to eat our packed lunches. We could get to know each other that way, she said, which meant that three girls talked to her out of politeness, the rest of the class became friends by taking the piss out of her outfit, and I was able to scoff my lunch in peace in and among a few autistic types at the edge of the group. I sat next to a boy with a fuzzy moustache and arms as thin as frankfurters, and together we didn't utter a word.

When, after my first week at St Odulf's, I came home crying, Dad said that you can't be bullied if you simply ignore the bullies. Two weeks later he bought a punchball.

'You must follow your fist,' he said, as he demonstrated a punch. 'As if you're punching right through the enemy.'

9

IN THE COMMON ROOM, I'm introduced to the other girls. There are so few. I mean, I knew this, but gathered together like this they look like a badly cast girl band. There are eight of them, and one has loads of tattoos and is wearing tracksuit bottoms, her hair in thick cornrows. Another has yellowish highlights with dark brown roots. Lots of piercings, a small, ugly nose. Those two stand out most. In between them sit the other six girls. So this is my group now. I scratch my head, and Geert, the supervisor who came to collect me, says my name. Then he points to them one by one: Henny, Geraldine, Soraya, blah blah blah. I don't know if I should shake hands or just sit down.

When I was on remand and they still thought I should go to a loony bin, I was placed among girls who'd been beaten up by their lover boys. They all shook my hand without looking at me and shuffled back to their rooms.

This lot here just stand there with their arms crossed. Only Henny, big and slow, holds out her hand. I raise a thumb and hate myself.

The table's laid with glasses, knives, loaves of bread, cheese, chocolate sprinkles and other shit to put on the bread. Six months of group breakfast, group lunch, group dinner. Six months. Everything about that sucks. Geert points to the table and we sit down. I sit down next to the girl with the tattoos. In prison movies the lead actor always turns out just to have perched himself in some corridor honcho's best friend's seat, and this is followed by a huge fight that teaches him that he has landed at the bottom of the food chain and has to earn the respect of the others. The girl with the tattoos says nothing when I pull up my chair. She smells of coconut oil and a conditioner that Miriam also uses and it catches me by surprise. She's wearing a Karl-Kani jumper on top

10

of tracksuit bottoms, its sleeves rolled up. Her lower arm has the face of a woman on it.

'Yo,' she says. She doesn't look at me. The others get on with grabbing chocolate sprinkles and pouring milk in their glasses and chatting. She takes white bread and opens a jar of peanut butter, spreads large dollops on her slices. Then she turns her face to me and lifts one eyebrow, the eyebrow tattooed with 'ONELUV' in florid letters, as if she wants to say: 'Excuse me?'

'Yo,' I say quickly and grab the Thermos that says it contains tea.

AFTER LUNCH I HAVE MATHS and Dutch and then geography in a classroom, the door of which also opens up to the interminable right-turning corridor. Not all the girls are in class. The teacher's a fat woman with a large, wooden necklace like the one Mum sometimes wears. She rattles off the text straight from the book, in all three lessons.

After geography I have time for one cig before we have to wait in our rooms for dinner. I turn left after smoking but end up in the common room instead of the corridor with our rooms.

'You have to be in your room in two minutes, so get a move on,' says Geert, tapping his watch. He's sitting at the dinner table, filling in some form. I sigh and walk the other way, past many doors, till I finally find my room. I hear how the others are playing music, rap and Natasha Bedingfield and Balkan pop, even when I slam the door shut behind me.

I look at myself in the mirror, touch the pink scar on my chin, lie on the bed, wait.

'Dinner time,' says Geert, opening my door. I trudge after him to the common room where a steaming pan of food is sitting on the table. Two girls set the table. The others are hanging on the sofas, at the table football table. I don't move from the doorway until the supervisors say we can sit down. I slowly make my way to the table, avoiding the girls who make for their usual places.

I sit down next to ONELUV again, at the end of the table, and she gives me a nod. I nod back. We eat bland macaroni with bits of carrot. The others are talking about a film with the supervisors, or, like me, spend most of their time looking at their plate. They try to pretend they're not looking at me. I, meanwhile, take in the space: two sofas, chairs, standard lamps, a cupboard with games, magazines, a table football table. One small desk with an ancient PC.

'This is only for girls who've been given permission,' Frits explained to me during the induction talk.

I keep thinking about it. That man. I have to ask. Not that I feel like being friendly, but I need to know. I eat and wait until the focus is no longer on me. Then I turn to ONELUV.

'Do they give you therapy here?' I ask. She frowns and takes a sip of water, swallows a spoonful of pasta.

'Yes, of course,' she says in a low voice. 'Why?'

'That dude that gives therapy, you know—'

'It's not a school subject or something.'

'Yes, no, right, but did you know that he—'

'Yes, *Hello Jungle*. You're not the first, man.' ONELUV shifts in her seat, wipes her mouth with the back of her hand. I turn my gaze to my plate again.

'But that dude,' I say after a while, 'it's not on, is it?'

'Yes it is,' she says. She prods a large piece of carrot with her fork. 'It sure is on. Just get used to it.'

After dinner some go back to their rooms and others wash up and clear away. ONELUV disappears. Someone turns on the TV. I decide to go to my room as well and unpack my things. I place my toothbrush and toothpaste next to the tiny basin behind my bed, clothes in the open cupboard by the window. My door's left ajar and I hear people laughing, walking back and forth, with someone taking a shower in the distance in the shared bathroom that Geert showed me. This is called free time. I can do what I like, within the rules of this place. I don't want to do all that much so I sit and wait, and I could phone home, but the idea that I'd have go to back to the common room makes me edgy, so I stay where I am and think, piss in the bog behind my bed, close the curtains and stare into the evening darkness until Geert calls in to say that the doors will be locked soon.

'Brush your teeth and go to bed,' he says.

When I'm finally in bed, I'm exhausted from doing nothing, dizzy. Geert comes by again to wish me goodnight, pulls the door shut behind him, peep, clack, and so I know I can start thinking. Get used to it, ONELUV said. My light's out. I left my watch on the bedside table, next to the lamp. I don't really understand what I should get used to. I wonder what Miriam will think of this, and Mum, Dad, Aunt Céleste. I listen to time's slow droning. Aunt Céleste cried when she heard the news. She cried straight into our living room via the speaker, like a girl, sob, snivel. I want this image to go away, but it won't. I'm floating in my own bed, that's how it feels, I can't move.

'Why should it end like this?' Aunt Céleste cries, loud and shrill, as if she's bent over my coffin looking at my dead body. I see her face above me, like a ball hanging from the ceiling. Her tears fall into my open eyes and mouth, taste salty, drip into my nose, choke me. Fat, sticky tears that end up in my eyes via my nose and then flow out again. I eventually turn my head away from Aunt Céleste, and my body wakes up with a start from the dream. I sit up, sweat on my forehead, my back. Then I remember: I'm here. Here.

I lie back and slowly calm down again. I gaze at the black void where the ceiling should be, where Aunt Céleste's head was suspended, close my eyes for more black and try not to cry, which I don't manage. My head's heavy and I think of grass.

'YOU'VE OVERSLEPT,' says the female supervisor who searched me yesterday. I have to get dressed and make my way to breakfast. 'We'll get you an alarm clock tomorrow. I'm Savanna, by the way. Without an h. Forgot to tell you yesterday with all that stuff going on. Up you get now!' She closes the door again. My body hurts, as if I've been lying in a cramped position all night. I get up, throw on some clothes, strap on my watch. Breakfast's officially nearly over and I feel shit. In about two hours I'll have been here twenty-four hours. One day will have passed out of the first month out of the six months I have to be inside.

FUCK FRITS. SERIOUSLY. The thing is, I know full well I'm not well. I'm the first to admit that shit. But it's a very strange punishment, I've decided. I can't keep myself in check.

'I'm not going to be helped by some fucking racist,' I screamed at him this morning, and Frits asked what on earth I meant.

I haven't always been like this, but since last summer, maybe a little longer, my head's been full of chaos. Like the alarm clock that Savanna put on my bedside table after the first day. I'm hoping that my alarm goes off and I simply wake up in another life. The other Salomé gets top marks for translations in Greek, is on holiday, plays the piano from memory, and I have landed in this very weird, parallel timeline in which I pick up a hole punch from Frits's desk during therapy and hurl it at the window. The glass didn't break because the windows don't just break here. I was so angry it didn't break that I shouted that I wanted to die. I'm becoming more dramatic by the day. It doesn't make any difference.

I'm only thinking in what Mum calls 'extreme terms' now, like when Miriam and I call each other fucking-this-or-that. I still don't know what came over me just now. The extreme terms fired out of my mouth like bullets. It comes without warning.

Frits called the supervisor, using the phone on his desk when I began to scream, and then Geert came running with Marco. I can't remember exactly what I did, but I'd been standing there under Frits's very nose and swearing and cursing. I went over to the hole punch and apparently picked it up again and this time I threatened to throw it at Geert, and he then wrestled me to the floor together with Marco, who threw me into my room, door locked.

Everything I do is in extreme terms. Because of these two big male bodies pressing down on me, my wrists and knees also hurt in extreme terms.

Now I have to stay here and I'm not allowed to go outside. Okay, I won't then. Just as Marissa thought it was a good idea to plaster her face with tattoos but is obviously the smartest out of everyone round here, I'm crazy, but I'm not wrong, am I? The shittiest thing about sitting alone in my room is that I've finished all my books. No distraction, only rotten shite in my head.

In prison movies men are always dying in isolation cells that are cold and dirty and have walls with all sorts of rubbish written on them. Here the walls are plain white, there's strip lighting and I can look out, but it's no fun, being on your own all day. I'm the kind of person that falls silent and starts to brood, Mum always says: stubborn. For a time, I was a fan of Joseph Gordon-Levitt from *3rd Rock from the Sun*, and I remember that once, when I was at home skiving and Mum and Dad were at work, I downloaded one of his films, *Manic*. In it, he's sent to a madhouse, not a prison. The therapist is a calm man, not a reality star who laughs at Africans. Maybe boneheads get angry when they reach puberty. Maybe there's a great deal to be angry about in my life. If this is the case, all this might be there for the long haul.

I'M NOT ALLOWED TO LEAVE my room until we have dinner. Marissa and Geraldine and Soraya, who's leaving next week, whoop when I enter. I shrug my shoulders and Marco says they should stop, that I should sit down. When we've finished eating and I'm washing up with Soraya, she says: 'Fuck that guy.'

'Yes,' I say. Soraya has long black hair that reaches down to her bottom. She's small; when she hands me a plate she has to reach upwards.

'Fuck all those motherfuckers here in this motherfucking shithole,' she says. She shrugs her shoulders at each word she utters. Soraya's on remand here. They're going to lock her up in a proper youth offender institute.

'No phone calls for you tonight, Salomé,' says Marco when I make my way to the phone room. I stop in the door frame.

'What?'

'Tomorrow. You can go and have a cigarette if you want, and then I want you to go back to your room.'

I open my mouth, but what difference would it make? I head off, to find Marissa. She's in the recreation yard. She shakes her head when I go outside and sit down next to her.

'What?' I ask.

'You're an idiot,' she says, blowing a smoke ring.

When I get back to my room I try to read, but instead I'm going over what Marissa said and what Soraya said, and I try to think what I really make of it myself, but it's not hitting me yet. I can't concentrate on my book. A single scream resounds in the corridor, and then loud music from someone's room. 'You're beautiful,' someone sings along, I think Geraldine. 'You're beautiful, it's true.'

SPRING HAS OFFICIALLY ARRIVED TODAY. In my dream I was standing in my parents' bedroom. Dad was kneeling at the foot of the bed. He was sweating while he was praying to God in whispers. The light falling on him, which made the beads of sweat glisten, reminded me of the last time I'd helped him spool a line around the reel of his fishing rod. That was the end of last summer, at the dinner table. In the yellowish light his sweat looked like golden honey. The drops trickled down from his forehead to the skin on his cheeks, where they remained. Then I saw Mum. She was sitting at the foot of the bed, staring straight out at the wall in front of her. Her hair was undone. It was long, so long that the ends reached the duvet. She was wearing an old-fashioned night-gown, like my grandma before she died.

'I'm sorry,' I called. I repeated it at least a dozen times. Each time Mum told me without looking at me that it was okay. It wasn't my fault. Those were the exact words I wanted to hear, but each time she said them I realised it wasn't enough. That it wouldn't change what I had done. Her voice sounded tinny, as if she was speaking over an intercom. And I knew that she could smell the blood of the dead body in my bedroom. I could smell it myself. It made me feel sick and I moved my hands to my face. And then I saw that they were red, wet. My knuckles on fire, their skin broken. I was naked, I was wearing a layer of blood.

Some mornings I wake up with my fingertips pressed against my neck as if I'm trying to pull off a necklace. This morning was no different. My nails were so deeply embedded in my throat that there was crimson blood underneath them. When I touch my neck it's burning.

I go to breakfast and then to school and then I wait in my room and then we have lunch and then I go back to school and then I go for a breather outside, all in a daze, as if I feel that, at any moment, someone might give me a huge fright. Up and down that curved corridor the whole time.

Today isn't a good day. I feel the need to talk to someone. Talk properly, like with Mum or Aunt Céleste. In my own words and in my own way. But I can't even think of trying that here. I understand it, but that doesn't mean I don't have a need for it, and that's shit.

On the way to the common room I pass Frits. He's holding a file in his hand. I know this because the folder has the same green colour as mine.

'I'd like to speak with you shortly!' he calls as he walks past me. He makes a pistol with his thumb and index finger and shoots. Then he mimes a bang noise with his mouth as if he's hit me.

'Whatever,' I say, but he's already walked on. I turn around and stick both my middle fingers up to his back disappearing around the corner, move on, kick open the door of the common room and see that it's empty. I drop down onto the sofa. It's starting to rain. I lean with my elbows on my thighs and rest my chin in the palms of my hands. I feel bad. I feel bad about everything. Everywhere. That business with the hole punch. The boringness of the lessons here. That sweet, repulsive deodorant the girls wear and you smell everywhere, if the reek of the lino floor or the sweat hasn't hit you first, that is. And cancer, I also feel bad about cancer. All types of cancer.

It was the end of last year, the end of 2007, that I picked up that you can see who's got it, if you know how to look. I saw it when I went to get doughnuts with Dad in the village, I saw it in his skin. It was one of the last days at home I had to prepare for my time here and the constant waiting during that period, the feeling that I had to sit absolutely still and look at everything with the utmost concentration, led to me actually seeing it, Dad's cancer. It's a layer, a complexion, it has a smell, it's in your bones. Once you've seen it you can no longer ignore it.

One of the first times I spoke to Frits, he asked whether I ever cried. Frits called me introverted. He also called me unpredictable and explosive. That we should deal with that. But I don't want him in my head. I'm not like Marissa. Only bad things make her head happy, she says so herself, that's why she needs help. She's not bad, but she gravitates towards the bad. I try to protect my head so that I can put together the pieces of the puzzle of the previous years, but Frits keeps jumbling them up with objectives.

I shift to the left-hand side of the sofa and the radio on the table next to it. The news. There are floods in Bolivia, loads of people died, and in parts of Africa there's meningitis. I wonder what my family are up to. Unlikely to be listening to the radio. Mum's at work; Miriam's in school, or skiving and smoking weed with Carlita. Dad might be watching the news on TV, seeing images of people in the Andes who're sitting on the roofs of their houses while the river's hauling away their sofas and cookers, or doctors in Burkina Faso who explain that they're still investigating whether it's a case of *viral* or *parasitic meningitis*.

Ashli and Feline enter the common room and sink into the other sofa, turn on the TV. Loud voices drive away the news on the radio. I get up and walk to my room. I lie down on my bed and try to read, even though the letters are swimming on the page.

When Frits comes to collect me with Marco half an hour later, I tell him to piss off. Marco stands in front of me, and says I shouldn't act so tough.

'You can't throw things at members of staff and you can't decide for yourself whether to go to therapy or not.'

Frits is standing in the doorway, arms folded, his grey ponytail over his shoulder, looking stern.

I won't, I continue to say, looking away from Marco, I won't, I won't, fuck it.

'That's not how it works here,' says Frits. 'If you don't do what you're being asked, it will have consequences for your visiting rights and temporary release procedure and—'

'Fuck you,' I say.

'I MAY GET OUT EARLY.' Marissa and I are sitting on the wooden bench under our building's awning. It's drizzling and cold. The drops are carried along by the wind, tepid and dirty on our trainers. Yesterday I spent the whole day in my room again, still because of the hole punch, because I don't want to talk to Frits.

'Wow,' I say. I rummage about in Marissa's coat pocket for her cigs. 'How come?'

'Don't know, man,' she says. She rubs with her hands over where her cornrows start. Then she grins. I think she's nervous, but you never know with her. Marissa's the only person I get on with. She says I'm lucky with what's hanging around here now compared to everything she's seen. She's in for a second time. I asked what she meant with the word lucky, and she then said that at least no one in the group has committed a real murder. Because, she said, that hits on the mood, you see?

Evidently what I did was something else altogether, however hard the public prosecutor tried to prove the contrary. I didn't really surprise Marissa at any rate.

'They say that if I'm prepared to talk to a psychiatrist, I can go on temporary release as a trial. So I can go and live with my mother sooner. I think I'm going to do that. My mum's going to agree,' she says, after blowing out a long line of smoke.

'Great,' I say. I light my cigarette, throw the package back into her lap. 'But won't you be stuck in some long pathway then? With a psychiatrist?'

'Perhaps. But it's the same here, though, innit?'

Marissa and I have been sitting next to each other at breakfast since the first week. When I don't sit down next to her, she joins me. Marissa's here for something to do with drugs and theft, she told me. I didn't ask any further. She's had many problems, she also told me, with her 'difficult family'. When she came out with that, I started to laugh. What, she asked, why are you laughing? I said she didn't need to say anything, that I didn't feel like talking either. That it's none of anyone's business. I think she liked that, that I said that.

Marissa lifts her legs and puts her feet on the bench. She wipes the drizzle from her face and looks at me.

'When you're out too we should go and hang,' she says.

'Yes.'

'Chill. In Eindhoven.'

'Yeah,' I say, 'sounds cool.'

Geert comes out. During the first week he tried to start a conversation with me about hip hop. He said I could maybe use the music room in the boys' unit. As an outlet, he said. His own inspiration was Tupac and Ice Cube, Nate Dogg. Marissa said that he'd tried that on her as well at some point.

'You're bright. With boys it also helps, making music. Give your problems a voice, rap about them, work with words.'

The thought alone makes me depressed. I said that I'd think about it.

It didn't happen, the music room, because they thought it was too big a risk for a girl to be in the boys' unit. When Geert said this, he looked truly disappointed.

Ashli later came up to me and said that she thought it was bullshit that I couldn't go to the boys' unit. Because, she said, who would want to rape you? I think she said that because I'm ugly. Or because I saw her ID card at one point, when she'd just come back from temporary release, and asked why her name was spelt wrong. I think she thinks that I think that her parents are stupid. According to Marissa she's a racist from the local trailer camp.

'Haven't you got anything better to do than to hang around?' asks Geert. He frowns at the cold, his hands in the pocket of his hoody.

'Nothing wrong with that, is there?' says Marissa.

'You're going to therapy in a bit, aren't you?' He nods at me.

'No choice.'

'Make sure you go this time, yeah?'

'Was I saying anything?' I get up and stub out my cig against the wall, throw it in the cig bin. Marissa stays put, so I head inside without saying goodbye.

When I'd just got here, I kept getting lost in the corridors. The building's circular, which is why we call it the Donut. The units are isolated from each other by secured walls, divided in such a way that each group occupies one of the Donut sections. We're in unit F, the boys in A to E. We never see them, although we feel their presence the whole time. The yard forms part of a smaller doughnut within the larger one: a circle with, every few metres, a smoking corner, demarcated by cement walls a metre thick. A metal gate connects the yards to the units and the sports court where you can play basketball, football, do fitness. You can sometimes hear the boys smoking in the other yards, but only dimly; their voices always far away.

We're never allowed to go onto the sports court on our own because there are more boys than us, because they're stronger. We're in the minority, as are the supervisors. The difference between us and the supervisors is that they alone have the authority and can say what we or the boys are allowed to do. If this is ignored, there are *consequences*. In a sense these consequences follow the logic of quicksand: the more liberties you try to take, the less room for manoeuvre there actually is to gain these liberties.

We can start to scream or hit someone or smuggle in weed, open our big traps. We can get angry about the punishment we're handed out for these things and go into endless discussions about what is or isn't fair, but this only lands you in isolation, and if you end up there you can't scream at or hit anyone apart from yourself, and even if you do that there are penalties. They make you stay longer.

Frits's office is a cubbyhole right next to the entrance of the unit. Your body drags itself there unwillingly because you want to do everything not to have to get anywhere near that bloke. As if someone expects you to lower yourself into a six-metre-deep

24

hole. When you sit down, the office feels large, because you're low down, while there's only just room for two chairs, a cupboard and a desk. In fact, it's a kind of cell, a cell disguised as an office, just as our cells are disguised as rooms. The tall wall to the right of the door is glazed and looks out onto the fencing that surrounds the Donut. This, as I discovered when I threw the hole punch, is made of toughened glass. It always smells of sweat here, Frits's, and the sour air from his rolling tobacco, the coffee he drinks all day. I had a chemistry teacher who smelled just like Frits and he died aged forty from a heart attack, the day after a test I failed. When I think about him, I see his skin, leathery, just like with Frits. All the moisture has been drawn away.

They believe that detention and therapy are the key to *rehabilitation*. In rooms like this, Frits's office, we youth delinquents are prepared for our 'return to society'. I think that's comical, I tell Marissa, because the last person who can prepare me for this is a prick who smells of death and spends his free time taking part in racist reality TV shows. That made her laugh.

The strange thing is that when you're here, you can almost taste freedom, as if you're waiting for a plane at the airport. The air's so thick and heavy and grey that you immediately begin to imagine what it's like to be away from here, how you'll cycle through the maize fields towards the villages, or along the meadows with cows and sheep, towards the city. And all those things only make you extra aware of the fact that you're not at all free. It's also because of Frits himself and the fence you see when you look through the window of his room.

He says I can trust him but I don't want to trust him.

'Whichever way you look at it, Salomé,' he says, 'at some point you will have to talk to me.'

I shrug my shoulders and look out of the window at the rain falling on the grass.

'And to try and have an open mind.'

'I'm here, aren't I?' I say.

'I'm also here for you.'

I look at him. He's leaning back in his big office chair. On his desk are a PC, a pen tray. There are papers. Half-turned towards me, as if someone who'd been sitting in my chair before had picked it up to have a look at it and then put it back, is a framed photo of a large Alsatian. The creature's sitting on a lawn. The frame is made of wood. I've not seen it before.

'You've got a dog,' I say.

'Indeed,' replies Frits. 'Do you?'

I take the frame and study the animal. It's young but definitely no longer a puppy. His mouth's open and his tongue's hanging out as if he's stoned and grinning. Somehow it really upsets me to see that Frits cares for a living creature.

'Do you celebrate the dog's birthday?' I ask.

'No. Does your family?'

'I never said I had one.'

Frits reaches with his hand across the desk. He wants the photo back.

I put down the frame and he takes it, turns it towards him. I annoy him, I think.

'I'd rather talk to you about how you feel than about my dog, do you understand that?' he asks.

'Yes,' I say.

'Shall we do that then?'

'I'm simply showing an interest, Frits.'

He laughs. Then the questions start, we have the chat. He asks me how the week went, whether I'd thought about what we talked about last time. He says it's important that I try and manage the anger that I feel differently. That I should give the people around me a chance. That they want to help me. That it's important that I allow myself to be helped. When he says the word 'allow', he bares his short, brown teeth. Aunt Céleste has small teeth and big gums, just like Frits. She has large, heart-shaped lips, almost brown. On the inside they're pink. As if inside her lips are raw, and fried on the outside. She once said, when I'd just gone to secondary school and we were videocalling, that it was important that I listened to my deepest self. That it's not about other people's rules but an 'internal logic'. She moved her long, thin fingers covered in gold

26

rings towards her head, as if she wanted to extract her thoughts from it and send them to me through the little lens above her monitor.

'You mustn't let yourself be taken for a ride,' she said in her fast French. 'You mustn't forget that there are forces working against you. You have to be aware of that.' I said yes. And she said no. She said: no, you don't understand, I've studied it, I've *studied*, very few people understand, the structures are turned against you, Salomé Atabong, it's important that you learn to deal with that. She said it's very normal if I feel that people don't have my best interests at heart. That I should act on that feeling when necessary, protect myself. Her eyes wide open, her dangling jewellery, her hair braided in so tightly that her eyebrows appeared pulled up by tension from the skin of her head.

'You can't just call someone a racist,' said Frits.

Aunt Céleste's someone who finds everything racist. From Cameroon's national debt to Spanish soaps. And if it's not racist, it's sexist. Aunt Céleste lives in Barcelona. Two years ago she was visiting a cousin in Paris, where she met a new man in a nightclub. It wasn't just any old man. He was a clever, caring, intellectual man, she said, who would make her happy in Spain, where he came from. She was still married to Uncle Honoré at the time, Dad's oldest brother. To be with this new man, she left Antoine, my cousin, behind in Cameroon and sent in the divorce papers paid for by her new man, who was heir to a Catalonian pastry manufacturer. The new man also financed her Philosophy studies at an English-language university. He's called Miguel and he's rich and old, just like Uncle Honoré when she married him.

Since she's been divorced, she hasn't stopped talking about feminism and colonialism, as if they're gods. The one good, the other bad. When we chat on the webcam – she talks into her headset and Miriam or I type without headphones in our poor French on MSN – she tries to give us advice. She says we should study and not let ourselves be betrayed by a man. Miriam always rolls her eyes afterwards.

'She's mad,' she once said. 'Just a gold-digger with a diploma.'

Dad thinks Aunt Céleste's a drama queen. Dad's the kind of person who says that working hard and not moaning are important. When he became unemployed he didn't use words like discrimination and racism.

Until a year ago I worked quite hard. I didn't really moan either.

'I don't just call someone a racist,' I say.

'I've never said or done anything racist in that show,' says Frits. He taps his pen against his coffee mug and gazes down to the floor, frowning. 'I've great respect for your culture, so that you know.'

'Which culture?' I ask. It starts to rain more heavily. In the strip lighting his skin appears papery, old, like dried-up skin on boiled milk. His grey irises contrast unhealthily with the yellowed white of his eyes.

'I know you can do much better than this,' he says, as if he hasn't heard me. 'So next time you'll simply be here when you're meant to be here, and don't throw things around. Understood?' I'm thinking of Mum and Dad and Miriam, and that I haven't spoken to them for two days. That they're worried, probably. I'm thinking very hard about this, very hard and deeply, and I say: 'Understood.'

Work hard. Don't moan. Then everything will always turn out okay, said Dad.

MAYBE THE DAY BEFORE YESTERDAY it wasn't such a surprise that things went wrong with Frits. Maybe I try and justify my behaviour because I find it difficult to look back and see what's really the issue. Looking back with honesty is difficult, more difficult than working hard. Don't moan.

'Now' is simply as it hits you, coloured by how you feel. Reminiscing is making up stories. But looking back and being honest is tricky. But it's got to be done, otherwise you won't learn to understand things. My thoughts have folded around themselves, just as the Donut encloses us day in day out. They swirl in and around each other. They're going nowhere, so I should look at them honestly, otherwise it'll never stop.

It went like this: Frits has been in Ivory Coast. And in Mali and Nigeria and South Africa and Zimbabwe and in Cameroon and in all the Northern African countries. He's travelled through the Sahara. A map of Africa hangs on the wall behind his desk. I hadn't mentioned this. There's a drawing pin in each country he has visited. When I first had to go to therapy he asked if I'd ever been in Cameroon. Because my name sounds Cameroonian.

'My name,' I say.

'Yes,' he says, with one of those laughs. The man from *Hello Jungle*, the programme that was on TV every Thursday night. I watched it, Dad half-snoozing after a football programme and me open-mouthed on the sofa. The man from the programme said: 'Your name sounds *Cameroonian*.'

He asked: 'Have you ever been in Cameroon, by any chance?' with such a fake-sympathetic voice, as if, on the basis of that question, we'd be able to create a bond or something, after everything I'd seen him do on TV. It made me instantly agitated. I love the word agitated, it's synonymous with irritated and it sounds like it feels: a-gi-ta-ted. *Tchak-tchak-tchak-tchak.*

'What's it to you?' I ask. And he pointed at that shit poster.

'As you can see I've done a bit of travelling in Africa.' I almost had to laugh. So I repeated my question.

'What's it to you?'

'I'm just interested.' And then I saw Aunt Céleste in my mind's eye, with all the gold around her wrists, the brightly coloured earrings, and that one long index finger that she prodded at her webcam. How slowly and clearly she said '*Nous sommes pas des animaux*' while next to me at the desk Miriam drank cola from a tea mug, sighing.

'If I've been there,' I said, 'even if that's the case, which is totally unimportant, by the way, are you going to ask me about my relationship with my family there? Or are we meant to connect over this? Because you've also been there?'

The disappointment on his face.

'I'm just asking a question. You don't need to answer it. I'm interested in your background.'

'And I'm simply asking a question in return,' I said.

He began to note down something in my file. I wanted to know what he was jotting down, but at the same I didn't want to know because he was probably writing something that had nothing to do with anything.

'Do you think I hit the boys because I come from Cameroon or something?' I asked. 'Well? I'm simply asking a question in return, Frits. Is that not allowed? Just say if not.'

Then Frits stared at me for a very long time.

'You did a bit more than hit them, didn't you?' he said. And that's when the whole thing started. I called him a racist, grabbed the hole punch and threw it against the window.

Perhaps it's stupid. Perhaps it's stupid that, only now that I'm thinking of Aunt Céleste, I have the courage to think about yesterday.

'She exaggerates,' Dad once said, and Mum said: 'Are you saying she's not right or something? After everything you've been through?' and Dad said: 'She grew up in Paris. She's wrong, she simply doesn't know what she's talking about,' and Mum: 'As if it's so great for them,' pointing at us, and Dad, sneering: 'They don't want for anything, do they?'

Don't want for anything. I don't want for anything.

I just mean to say that sometimes I don't know why things hit me so badly. When Dad talks about his youth, I get the impression that I should keep my mouth shut. When Dad, who grew up when the French 'were still in charge', isn't angry, then I shouldn't be either. So angry it surged out of my body. It's too stupid. It's boring and stupid how it's all panned out. Predictable and low and stupid.

'When they hit, *always* hit back,' he said when at one point I came back crying from school, where in addition to me (I counted) there were four other 'foreigners': three Chinese and a Turkish kid. But when I told him why I cried he said: 'Fists hurt, you're stronger than words, aren't you?' He shrugged his shoulders.

Dad thinks that if someone calls you a fucking nigger, you should respond with high grades. Not that an A in Dutch has ever given me the fabulous feeling that some classmates seemed to have when they called me a monkey.

Perhaps it's only a way of bringing up children, fending them off from your own mistakes, correcting through them the things you've done yourself.

It would obviously be weird if Dad said: 'Fists hurt, and when someone calls you fucking Africans you throw them through a café window or kick off their car's wing mirror.'

Which is what he did himself.

THE FIRST PILE OF BOOKS Mum brought along for me included *The Old Man and the Sea*. I found it such a depressing book that I threw it into the bin. The tone, the fisherman's homecoming with that fish's skeleton and the fact that those tourists don't understand what the skeleton stands for. I was close to tears. But I said that I liked it, when she asked me. Because I could tell that she wanted me to be impressed. I hope she will bring along something that cheers me up, which doesn't put the idea into my head that everything is pointless. I think that often enough as it is.

Mum is old. An elderly mother. She's already fifty-three. She also gives me old books, instead of a comb. My hair's a disaster. When I pull out the elastic from my bun it just stays there, all curled around itself.

Old literature is what she brings. Translations of French writers and books about sad women from the last century. My Dutch teacher believes there's a difference between *literature* and *reading matter*. Reading matter is cheap entertainment, he said. You, you, he very slowly panned his gaze around the class, are the four per cent who are going to make the difference in our society. We had to read *Reynard the Fox* or the one book by Piet Paaltjens. Someone asked if *Lord of the Rings* was literature as well, and my Dutch teacher laughed at him. It also took him half a lesson once to explain the difference between 'cheap' jokes and humour. He said that stupid people like coarseness, funny voices and fart jokes. Coarseness, he repeated with the tips of his index fingers bent against his thumbs so that the four fingers formed a circle, doesn't require any *intelligence*. People who are clever, who are educated, like real humour, clever humour, intelligent humour, such as satire. Then he explained the difference between irony, cynicism and sarcasm.

Four per cent. I wonder how many out of that four per cent end up in here. Maybe I'm the only one, the exception to a shitty rule.

If I've learned anything over the past year, both at school and at home, it's that things simply happen and that clever people can be just as stupid as stupid people. That working hard and not moaning isn't enough. It doesn't make you invisible. You continue to be a target.

So I'm hoping for a book that tells me something other than everything I already know, everything I want to throw into the bin because I can't bear it.

Mum and Miriam are already waiting for me when I enter the visitors' room.

'Oh, the queen has arrived,' I say to Miriam when I slam the door shut behind me.

'I can go, you know,' she says. Mum places a hand on her leg.

'How are things? What have you been doing?'

I tell her what I've been doing while Miriam stares at the water cooler in the corner, arms folded.

'Oh honey,' Mum says, 'oh honeybunch.'

'I get it,' says Miriam. 'Let the bitch learn a lesson.'

'Language!' Mum snaps at her and then gives me an imploring look. 'It's important you try to allow yourself to be helped, don't you think?'

'I'm really doing my best,' I reply, 'but that man makes my fucking blood boil.'

'And quite right too,' says Miriam, still not looking at me.

'Yes, but try and let him do his work, because he's trying to help you get rid of your anger.'

'Where's Dad?' I ask, because I don't want to have this discussion. Miriam throws Mum a sideways glance.

'He didn't feel too good,' she says.

'Chemo pills,' says Miriam.

'It affects his bowels.'

'But the tumour's shrinking, right?' I ask, and Miriam shrugs her shoulders.

'We don't know yet.' Mum takes a sip of water from the plastic cup she's holding in her chubby hands. 'He worries about you.'

'There's no need.'

'Maybe it would help if you tried *not* to attack people instead of actually doing it. I'm sure it'll make him sleep better.'

I stare at the ceiling.

'How on earth's Frits going to teach me not to attack people?' I ask.

'That's a good question,' says Miriam. Mum rests her fingertips against her eyebrows, the way she does when she has a headache or tries to add up some numbers.

'How are things going at school?' she then asks.

'I already know everything.'

'So no Greek.'

'I'm doing a lower stream or something.'

'Are you making any effort at all?'

'Yes, I'm making a huge effort.'

There's nothing as boring as pretending that I haven't had to work out these mathematical formulas before, but because homework's so easy, at least it gives me time to read after school. I ask about my comb and Mum says 'shit' and Miriam flips her braids over her shoulders. They are red this time, with golden hair bands at the ends.

'You could shave it all off.' She grins and I stick up my middle finger. Mum talks about the woman next door who's forever popping around with homeopathic books that say that Dad should eat green peppers to make his tumour shrink.

'She thinks you can eat away your cancer,' says Miriam. 'Stupid woman.'

'He pretty much kicked her out of the house.' Mum starts to laugh and Miriam and I join in.

'I hope he can come next week,' I say.

'Yes,' replies Mum and her laughter fades.

Up until visiting time's over Miriam talks about Carlita who's due in two weeks, and Mum asks me what I thought of the Hella Haasse book she'd given me last time. I report back and she says she has more books by her, if I'd like, and I say that I'd like that. When Marco knocks on the door to say that we should finish off, we all get up at the same time and Mum gives me a hug. Miriam stretches her hand, grubs about in my bun with her fingers and pulls my knotted hair. It hurts.

'Jeez, Salomé,' she says.

I STACK THE BOOKS on my bedside table and sit down against the wall, diagonally across the mattress. I gaze at nothing, at white, a blank, streaks of paint and bumps in the concrete. I have no posters, no letters, no cards. I don't tally the days, nothing. When, after a visit like that, I'm going over things in my head, I don't think about the people here, they don't interest me. I don't even think about Marissa. I just think about the past: about days at the seaside with Mum, Grandma and Granddad, the time Miriam got lost in Madurodam, how Dad once came down in Mum's big floral pyjamas and a shower cap during breakfast, put on a Prince record, strumming air guitar until Miriam and I were in such stitches that Miriam sprayed tea from her nose. When I think about that I become happy and calm and I think: things will work out okay.

But I then somehow always get to the other shit: Dad and Mum's fights, Grandma's death, followed by Granddad's, all kinds of other nasty shit: the day at school that Salvatore threw bananas at me, the first time I stole a phone from a classmate, the meadow, the police. This is the thought I get stuck in the longest. Every detail of every event that brought me here I see in front of me, until I feel sick and start to read until the nausea disappears. It doesn't always.

MUM'S RIGHT. It would be better if I turned my mind to things other than Frits van Gestel. For me and for Frits and for the blood pressure of the people I love. I think it's because I find it too absurd. I really do think it's absurd. I'm not being a toughie or anything. I don't want to be anyway. I just had to make it clear to him that it's absurd that I find myself in one single space with him, that the clock has started ticking in such a way that he has to help me with something he so obviously doesn't understand. I don't think it's remotely funny either. I scream because I don't want to cry. And then it all goes wrong.

I mean, I should think it through more thoroughly. Perhaps I should try to understand. Get used to it, said Marissa. Which is strange. I'm used to so much shit already.

I remember when I was thirteen, I had just gone to secondary school and was smoking cigarettes I had stolen from Dad from my bedroom window. More than anything, I was imitating what Miriam did. Inhale, hold smoke in my mouth and blow out. I downloaded an album by an artist I had discovered via Myspace and put that on and would then smoke ciggies with a towel wedged against the gap under the door. It was something like half past eleven that evening and Miriam had gone AWOL again, for a change. She'd been sneaking out the whole time, and when she came home she would have a fight with Dad and he would hit her sometimes. I don't know what it was, but she was constantly in trouble, especially with boys. It made us all nervous, Mum could really swear in those days.

The bus came from Tilburg along the B-road, the road our house looked out onto. It stopped at the bus stop and Miriam got off. She halted for a moment to smoke a cigarette, I think, and then a car popped up behind the departing bus. The car pulled over, a boy got out, and she began to argue with him. His voice was very low. It echoed. At first I just carried on smoking, but then he began to pull her arm, and she pushed him away, and he pulled and called her a slag. Miriam hit him in the face and they kept fighting for a long time. Their screams were piercing, ugly. It needed to stop. Then another boy got out of the car and I wanted to shout to warn her but I realised just in time that I really shouldn't do that because Dad and Mum were at home, what if they heard it, but he started to yank at Miriam's other hand, the boy with the low voice grabbed her by the throat, so then I jumped out of the window, into the tree that was in front of the house and I held on to one of the branches and slid my feet against the trunk and with my one hand I held on and with the other I grabbed the last branch, dropped myself, and one way or another climbed down. I ran towards Miriam, to the bus shelter with the tiny, ancient car with the boys in it and to the boys who were beginning to pull her into the car and then I screamed something and they got distracted and Miriam punched the boy with the low voice on his nose and shouted that we should get a move on, 'Come on, hurry!', and we ran away into the neighbourhood. She was extremely frightened and so was I.

She had to cry and didn't stop saying goddammit goddammit shit and I had burnt my arm with my cigarette when I jumped out of the window into the tree and I didn't know if Dad and Mum had heard anything. I mean, I jumped into a tree and climbed down it. I . . .

We kept listening out for a car, but it was quiet in the street. All we heard was our breath and the rustling of cats in the bushes. Miriam's hand hurt and there was a twig in my shirt and lots of those caterpillars that live on birch trees during the spring in my hair. Miriam railed at the boys, whom she knew, she said, 'I never thought he'd do something like *that*,' and I asked her what it was he was going to do, but she wouldn't say. She grabbed her cigarettes from her trouser pocket, but they had snapped and then she smacked them on the ground and they were bastards, she hated them, she hated all the boys at school and in this shit village.

'We should go back,' she said all of a sudden. It was a Thursday, I still remember. She whispered it, it was that quiet. We went into the garage via the passages between the back gardens and slipped back into the house. Very quietly through the kitchen. Very quietly in the hallway. Everything dark and by touch with Dad snoring and an action film playing. We had almost got to the attic stairs when Mum came out of the bedroom and she looked at me and she looked at Miriam and said nothing. Her face silver because of the moonlight, her greying hair in a bun on her head.

We never talked about it since. So that's one of those things I could think about for months afterwards. In order to get my head around it. I reconstructed it fully, what must have happened and why. What could have happened. A kind of CSI. I also asked Miriam, later, when we were doing the dishes, what exactly had happened, before I jumped into the tree, but she said, everything was fine in the end, wasn't it? 'It's finished between us. Everyone's safe and everything's okay,' she said, and pushed a wet pan against my stomach. 'Stay out of it.'

But everything was not okay. We never talked about it since, but it was during the same period as Dad's punchball and my tears when I came home from school. I don't know what he knew, but he took Miriam and me to the garage and lugged the stand with the ball on it from the wall.

'I'm going to teach you how to defend yourselves,' he said.

Perhaps that evening was the last straw. Perhaps it was a coincidence and Mum hadn't told him anything.

Miriam thought the punchball was stupid but I had seen Dad have a fight with the neighbours, knew that a show of strength could be effective. And I didn't stay out of it. I just had to put the jigsaw pieces together to figure it out. Every detail, the feeling of birch bark against the palm of my hand, the boy's hand on her throat, her whack, the squeaking tyres of the car, the screaming in the night, as we ran through the streets.

When I came home from school I would go to the garage and when Dad came home from work and found me there, he would turn on the radio, smoke and give instructions.

'It's obvious where you got it from,' said Mum.

Everyone's safe and everything's okay.

'It's important that you don't let anyone mess you about,' Dad said, showing me how to punch. 'You step forward with your jab. As if you're punching right through the enemy.'

Through them. Be powerful. Speed. Work hard. No moaning. Don't be messed with.

And if it does happen: move with surprising speed.

That was the goal.

FRITS NEVER SAID ANYTHING I could actually label nasty. I'm too judgemental, as Miriam sometimes says. Because I roll my eyes, and instead of reacting to things, let a long silence fall, or the opposite, and start screaming. But what I don't do is nothing. The thing is that I *do* react. In the end. With surprising speed. I jump into a tree if necessary and I clamber down it without thinking. Perhaps that's not the way it should be.

When, three times in a row, instead of going to Frits's office I went to my room to read, Geert tells me I've got to go and see the director.

'You've skipped enough sessions,' he says, opening my door and placing his hands on his hips. 'I've found you here for the third time when you should be somewhere else.'

'I can't do it,' I say, putting my book to one side.

'You have to.'

'I don't have to do anything.'

'Yes, but that's the thing about being here,' says Geert, 'you most definitely have to.'

THE DIRECTOR EXPECTS ME the following day after lunch. Marissa laughs at me during PE. We run in circles around the recreation yard clutching a stopwatch to time ourselves. A miserable-looking Henny's sitting on the side with a yellow water bottle, her face bright red, her heavy breasts moving up and down with every fast puff of breath.

'I don't think you get the actual idea, man,' says Marissa while we overtake Feline and then Ashli.

'I'm not going,' I repeat.

'Believe me, you will.' She puts on a sprint to be tough and, while I finish my circuit, I think about it. With her braids streaming behind her she appears to be flying around the yard, as fast as a car that's almost going off the road on a bend.

'Am I the only one who finds it too fucking much that we get therapy from someone who's been on TV?' I ask, when Marissa runs alongside me again, panting.

'No.'

'What is it then?'

Marco, who's standing in the centre with Savanna, blows a whistle and we can stop running.

'Hand your stopwatch in first!' he calls, and we go over to Savanna, who collects the stopwatches in a small box. Marco begins to take balls out of a net and throws them at four girls, one of whom is Marissa. She stops the ball with her instep.

'I think you're the only who's here for a hate crime, or something?'

'It wasn't a fucking hate crime.'

'But you do hate them?'

'Dude.'

Just like the others, we go and stand opposite each other and kick the ball back and forth. Every time I kick the ball at Marissa she tries a trick, all kinds of difficult shit I really don't feel like, and then she heads or kicks the ball towards me. Henny's got up and, because we make odd numbers, she's playing with Savanna.

'It wasn't a hate crime. I just wanted them to stop,' I say.

'I'm not judging you!' Marissa calls as she cradles the ball in her neck and makes a few jumps, three four five times, before it drops and she manages to manoeuvre it between her legs with a casual toe clip. 'If I got treated like shit at a white shite school like yours I'd also go para. And on top of that, Fuckface van Gestel as therapist?'

'Yes, that,' I say.

'Just say that you're sensitive. Show emotion,' she says. She prepares to kick the ball, comes running for it, but instead of giving it a full thwack, she only gives it a soft tick, scoops it up in the air and holds it high.

'Finish up!' Marco roars and he blows hard on his piercing whistle. There's swearing. I put my hands on my ears. Marissa grins and, while heading the ball, rolls up the sleeves of her sports sweater. The tattoo of her Mum's face stares at me from the inside of her arm.

'You don't get it, man. You mustn't make it so difficult for yourself. When you start crying you don't get punished, right,' she says, and she lets the ball bounce on the recreation yard's tarmac and then kicks it to me. I duck too late and it hits my stomach hard.

'Fuck!' I shout.

Marissa cackles with laughter.

'Cry, bitch!'

THE DIRECTOR SITS in his big, bold office with his big, bald head and lets his lower arms rest on the desk top.

'If you carry on like this you won't be allowed any more phone calls,' he says.

'Yes, but . . .' I start, but he raises his hand.

'Then we suspend your visiting rights, then your temporary release is paused, and if you continue to refuse, no evening activities, no recreation time, your sentence will be extended, isolation cell, and that's not all. You're not here for fun, right?'

I look away from him because I immediately start to boil.

'We have the power to restrict your freedom up to the number of showers you're allowed to take, madam. That's not something you'd want, I take it.' His eyebrows shoot up. I'm sitting in an uncomfortable chair opposite him and try to keep my face straight, not to frown, not to get up and not to spit in his face.

'As a matter of fact, why don't you go?' he then asks.

'Because he makes me angry,' I snarl.

'And why does he make you angry?' Again those eyebrows. He looks like he's been in the army and eaten a lot of meat. A closed look in his eyes. He's dressed in a lumberjack shirt, like Dad sometimes wears. Just about the opposite of the head at my school, with her expensive suits and complicated necklaces.

'Because I can't talk to him,' I start, and my voice betrays me, trembles, 'because he—'

'Has been on TV, yes.' The director sighs, and he rubs the palm of his hand over the edge of the table top.

'On that *programme*.'

'That programme, yes.' He looks tormented Perhaps Marissa's right. It's just that I've never tried to cry at will. I clear my throat and try to stay calm.

44

'In view of the nature of my offence,' I say solemnly, 'you might be able to understand—'

'Yes,' he replies sharply. He hits the table with his enormous hand. The fat ring around his ring finger makes a loud noise on the surface. 'Of course I can understand that. But what you have to understand is that Mr van Gestel is a qualified therapist. This is no holiday resort, Ms Atabong. You're here to serve a sentence, and part of that sentence is therapeutic support. This isn't something you have a say in or can express a wish about. So this is as good as it gets for now.' He stands up. I've only just got here. I had really expected a longer sermon.

'For now?' I ask, rising.

He pulls a face as if he has swallowed something nasty. 'Well,' he says, and is quiet for a moment.

I try to produce a tear with all my might, but then he waves me off.

'To your lesson, and no more shenanigans. You can forget your visit this week. Hopefully you'll learn from this.'

'But—' I begin.

'Off with you.' He makes his way to the door, opens it and gestures for me to go. 'Tomorrow you'll be in Mr van Gestel's office again, and that's that.'

So off I go. I stamp right and right and right until I get to the common room where I find Marco filling in some form with Feline.

'And?' he asks. Feline stares awkwardly at the paper, chewing the pen in her hand.

'Well, you know,' I say.

'Just get yourself to your lesson then, quickly,' he says. 'And tomorrow, be on time at Frits's.'

I leave the common room and head for the classroom. No fucking visit, and tomorrow I will have to sit facing that fucking shyster's shitty grin. When I enter, the map of the world has been rolled out in front of the blackboard. The map is big and old, yellowed, and compared to other continents Africa suddenly seems so tiny.

SO NOW I'VE GOT TO UNDERSTAND. Okay, then I will understand. I'd quite like to know why, as it happens. Perhaps it was
a producer from a commercial TV channel. I'm thinking a few
years back, 2004, spring. I was still at primary school. I have to
understand that that producer thought: brilliant idea. I have to
understand that he thought: fucking cool, that he had something
to prove. I have to understand and understand, and as I said, it's
pathetic, it's boring. I think it must've gone something like this;
that producer, who has thought up the whole thing, had never
managed to get one of his ideas onto the box. His colleagues
don't like him. He's lagging behind them. He wants to score. He
wants people to recognise him when he enters a bar, wants them
to come and ask to shake his hand, while he takes a moment to
determine whose handshake he'll accept. That's what he wants. I
can understand that.

So I imagine one of those grey meeting rooms. There he is
with his wired, coffee-swigging colleagues. They're brainstorm-
ing. That's what it's called. It's quite a business. Whiteboards
are scrawled on with black markers, Post-its fly through the air.
There's a great deal of foul language. These people make TV. They
decide what the nation will talk about around the water cooler at
work, over lunch, on the radio. They work with stars. They are
important. Their target audience? Working people who want to
relax on the sofa with a bottle of beer and a bag of crisps on the
coffee table in front of them. These are the people they entertain.
Blah blah blah. I can get that bit.

They are looking for something outlandish, something really
incredible, something that makes you both laugh and cover your
mouth with your hand. Something so excruciating it becomes
hilarious. The man with the golden idea, the guy who wants to

46

score, is probably called Floris or something, but we call him Golden Idea. Golden Idea is without doubt a colleague of the dude who thought up *Let's Get Dressed!*, the programme in which adolescents swap clothes and make-up and then have to go out. The episode with the goth from Ede who had to swap outfits with the Antillean rapper from Schiedam was a scream. We laughed: ha ha ha. Look at them. Big leather coats and shirts with dragons exchanged for gold fake teeth and Fucci trousers. And then the posh airhead from 't Gooi who had to swap with a gay boy from Apeldoorn: powder and heels and pop music everywhere.

The woman who makes blubber TV is also in this grey meeting room, with her *Big Brother* meets *From Trouble to Angel* show: *A Last Chance*. Whole families in rehab with their addicted sons and daughters and fathers and aunts. Coke, heroin and weed-addicted students who have a relapse in front of their parents. Fathers who do a runner from the clinic to go to the pub. Mothers who steal credit cards to use them during the sales. And all on camera. I watched it too. It even affected me once, making me shake my head and think: how awful, how awful. So I get it, I really do.

So, there they are. I'm imagining them eating doughnuts, or is that too American? Maybe just gingernuts or shortbread. Or something like almond croissants. Maybe cake. Yes, it was someone's birthday, so it's cake. Brought along from the kitchen, with the cups of coffee and tea, on a napkin. They use their fingers to eat it, cause you shouldn't make such a big deal of it. Thursdays. When everyone stays longer. When the best ideas come up. Then to the pub. White wine and bread with a dip if there's any room for that.

The guy I'm talking about, Golden Idea, has probably tried everything: survival programmes and reunion talk shows and DIY TV. The others found it all too earnest. Whatever the fuck that may mean. But he has come to work prepared today. It's a bit strange really that he hadn't come up with it before, looking back on it. It's insane no one's had this idea before, he thinks, wolfing down his slice of cream cake in three bites. It's so extremely obvious, after all. The golden idea hit him on the tram on the way home, a few days ago. Now I really have to use my imagination, but I suspect a flat in Amsterdam-West. The newer part, so quite a way out. Flat tyre, so instead of cycling along the canals to the station, he was trapped on that rank tram. It was raining; he was pondering, perhaps a holiday to escape the rut. His girlfriend's at uni. Always stuck in books, often in the library, more often at home, on her laptop at the dining table with a blanket over her shoulders. *Anthropology*. From anthropos and logos: the study of people, I remember from Classical Studies and Greek. Not exactly a field he understands why you'd get into. All those bare-titted tribes in those jungles. All exotic bullshit. And does it pay for her living? his father would ask with raised eyebrows. And he knows how he can reply to that with his own raised eyebrows. But whatever, that's not what it's about. She's so cute when she's sitting there studying with her hair in a bun and glasses, how you could not fall for that? But maybe I'm filling in too much detail now.

That girlfriend, she studied rituals in the blahdeblah in Angola or somewhere. Perhaps it was the Incas? Who cares. Whatever it was, she was interested in all those men in Africa, those young dudes who jump over bulls and hack off their foreskin and drink sour milk in the forest for a week and then hallucinate. That shit. Sweat lodges and public sex. A kind of *Ace Ventura: When Nature Calls*, but then for real. It was quite interesting – at times. But more than anything, comical, really. He usually didn't fancy it, all that yakking on about those blacks, but every now and then, when he'd been to the pub after work and come home, and she would tell him about the chapters she'd written, the work about her research trip that summer which she was reading through again, then it was actually really gripping. A kind of farce. It's funny, isn't it? From our cool, Dutch perspective, he would say, all that piss drinking's more than anything, in fact, in all honesty, simply so weird that you can only howl with laughter.

She didn't like that, of course, when he said it for the first time. She took it all extremely seriously. Brought figurines back from Namibia and went on a desert trip with a girlfriend. She went on safari, slept under mosquito nets and in clay huts in the Congo.

Or was it Namibia after all . . . Angola? And then he would start to knock it. But the more it happened, the more she got used to it. She would sometimes even laugh along with him. She could see his point. And what's more: how would the Bamileke or Tonga people react when they saw what weird things we get up to here in Europe? Ha ha indeed, a lot of laughter. That's how I imagine those two at their dining table in their flat. But it got him thinking, his girlfriend's obsession. Because he's obviously not the only person who responds to sagging tits and animal bones in hair and to those village elders with their sticks and drinks that make you see stars. The average Dutch person wouldn't know what to do with that, would they?

So. Some time in 2004, I think. On a Thursday morning after the cake. The golden idea. He can see it in front of him, there in the meeting room. He can smell it. Today, as they say, he'll take fate into his own hands. Today he's going to score. That's how it went, I think. I can really imagine it.

The meeting's in full swing. Someone suggests a dating show in which physically and mentally disabled people have a blind date. That already exists, says someone. Then we let them go on survival as well, says someone else.

'No,' the channel controller says, who's just arrived, coffee mug in one hand, mobile in the other, his shirt tightly tucked into his trousers. He's bald, his head as shiny as a mirror. He flops down into a chair next to a producer and gazes at the whiteboard. He raises his eyebrows as he takes another sip of coffee.

'I really think—' his producer whimpers.

'Rubbish. People like Downies, no way will we let them go orienteering. Can you imagine the shitstorm that would hit us if one of them breaks an arm? Bad for the channel's image. Other ideas?'

Colleagues exchange nervous glances. It's all a big laugh with cake served and feet on the table until the boss enters.

'*Other. Ideas*,' he repeats.

'I had something with—' the group's dunce kicks off. Mr Golden Idea can't take it any longer. That he and the section's dunce are on the same score as far as accepted pitches are concerned (zero) is his biggest frustration. But he calms down. Today his life's going to change, remember.

'Yes, well . . . it's somewhere on the board,' the dunce splutters. There's still a bit of whipped cream on his wrist, the dickhead, and he squints at the whiteboard. His glasses are in his hair, but there's no one to give him a hand.

'Too long!' Boss thunders. Everyone starts. Some snigger. 'All the time you just sit here eating yourselves silly, time I pay for, goddammit, but when I come in no one! Ever! Has! An! Idea!' The mug's slammed onto the table. The coffee sloshes over the edge. The producers sink themselves back into the hard backs of their chairs, suddenly check messages on their phones with the utmost focus, check that they don't still have cake crumbs on their clothes somewhere. But Golden Idea fixes his gaze on the Boss. His shiny crown. His hairy fingers still curled around the mug's handle.

'Anyone?' Boss sighs.

He waits a moment. A momentary silence, disappearing into it.

'Incredibly. Sad. Do you know what's at stake here? In addition to your jobs, of course, because they're obviously at stake, I can tell you. Do you know how many people would kill for your jobs? How many recently graduated interns I could easily—'

Everyone knows he's having a whale of a time. Boss digs these sermons. The sweat breaking out. The smell of fear and self-hatred. Halfway through the tirade Golden Idea raises his hand.

'What?'

'I've got something, I guess?'

'I guess?'

'Yes, I was thinking,' says Golden Idea, as if he's shy, but he isn't really, of course, 'maybe, yes, maybe it's really crazy.'

'Spit it out, man.'

'Well, you've got those exotic travel programmes, you know.'

'Expensive!' someone behind him shouts. But he doesn't appear to have heard it. Boss waits.

'And then it's always some kind of scientist or expert or experienced traveller who goes into the forest or talks to people in developing countries, swims with dolphins, feeds monkeys, you know the kind of thing.'

'Yes. The Michael Palins of this world. That's National Geographic material,' says Boss.

'And Discovery, in fact,' says Golden Idea. Sighing, clicking pens. He will not let himself be discouraged. 'But that's not the point. The point is that if you want to learn something about these places it makes really great TV. If you want to get to know more. From some kind of fake-anthropological bullshit perspective from a presenter who's far too clever or a biologist with a winning smile. It's always people who know far more than the average viewer who do these kinds of shows. Right? And this got me thinking. What does the average viewer think of those far away places? Themselves? Not based on the Michael Palins and those biologists?'

Now he has captured everyone's attention. Boss is still casually leaning back in his seat, but his fingers are now clasped around the handle of his mug, his eyes like fishhooks in the flesh of Golden Idea's brain.

'So, what if we let the average viewer decide for themselves what they think of the jungle?' Boss is even starting to grin, dammit. He hears someone swearing behind him at the table. 'With a camera crew and an interpreter. Or perhaps not, perhaps no interpreter. Just a fun couple flying to Burkina Faso or Madagascar or Mali. In any case, a place where they're still going around in banana skirts. We immerse them for two weeks in the traditional way of life of those African tribes and then they have to do everything they do: wash clothes, scoop cowshit, cook goat stew, all that shit. We link up with travel organisations in those countries. No such thing as bad publicity. Our guinea pigs have to attend the rituals, worship their gods, sleep in the same hammocks. They must let their own Dutch children play with those little ne—'

'Hoho,' Boss bellows with his free hand in the air, 'we call them *Africans*, right?'

'Sorry, sir,' says Golden Idea, 'play with those Africans, *Africans*. With sticks and car tyres or whatever they do over there, instead of PlayStation. We stir it up a bit, there in the jungle. No interpreter, no, it's better like that, as little communication as possible, and then we get them back home after two weeks and put the whole thing together.'

Silence has fallen in the meeting room. Golden Idea's still panting after his pitch. For a moment, he swears he saw it, he *was* simply there, in Africa, with his volunteers, his crew, the heat of the sun. I don't want to interrupt, don't want to steer, but I believe he truly astonished himself. He wanted that promotion, sure, but no one, least of all himself, thought he had it in him. Appeal to the average viewer. The cultural veneer over the show. The *comical* aspect. Exotic. All those things together. By thinking about it like this I try to understand it. And perhaps it's not honest, and I'm now making something of this that it isn't. But I'm doing it, just as they are. Because look: Boss is staring at him open-mouthed. His colleagues are coming out with expletives again, and this isn't stopping. Everyone knows what has just happened here. What kind of miracle they're witnessing. This is one of those moments in your career, one of those fucking brilliant days you think back on later, in the car on the way home. One of those moments about which you can say: 'It was gold' or: 'I did that', and that that was the truth. Boss licks his lips and takes another sip of cold coffee. His mouth doesn't even twist. The cogs are turning.

He gets up so quickly that Golden Idea and three others leap up at the same time.

'Work it out. And get a move on. I want you all to work on this like the clappers so that I can present it next week. I'm thinking March, yes March, we'll start filming in March. Is that feasible?' A short pause in which everyone's gasping for breath. 'Fuck it, make it feasible. We're going to Africa, guys. Don't forget your Jungle Juice!' Boss storms out, en route to the next meeting. Golden Idea's still standing there, eyes fixed on the whiteboard, his prick half-hard by now. (Or is that corny? Too easy?)

Maybe no history was written, maybe it was far less epic. Maybe they just banged some ideas on the whiteboard and this was the only one that stuck, they made a few phone calls, it grew into an idea until it was suddenly there. I don't know. I don't really need to know.

Two weeks later there's a casting call, a call for down-to-earth volunteers 'who don't lack curiosity for other cultures'. A man with a badly trained Alsatian scrolls through the criteria on the website. He glances at the small globe next to his desk in his flat in Breda. Africa's turned towards him, with pins in the countries he's visited over the past few years, positioned next to his framed Beingabletodosomethingwithdifficultchildren university certificate. (Or is that too easy again? Perhaps the certificate's simply lying in a drawer. Perhaps he has no globe, but he's simply staring out of the window, or into the kitchen where the washing up is waiting next to the sink.)

So the man's staring. And he sighs. And he imagines the scene. It cheers him up, the idea. He opens his mail, types a response. Or he sends a letter. That's boring. He'll tell his girlfriend later. She'd always wanted to join him on one of his trips to Africa. Maybe he can sell it to her as a surprise holiday? Why not? It's good fun, isn't it? Aren't they a prime example of ordinary, down-to-earth viewers? This is their chance.

When I conceive it like this, when I imagine it, then I can understand it. Then I can visualise how it ended up like this. And that makes me calm. Not the kind of calm I get dangling my legs out of the window and listening to music, but the kind of calm that comes over me when I ask a question in correct Dutch in the supermarket and this takes people aback and I know exactly why. You don't need to explain to me that things can take a very odd turn. And maybe it's not right that I regard this with such a *cynical* outlook. But I'm cynical because my fate is so *ironic*. The point is that I understand it, I understand it very well. I'm an ace at understanding things. I work hard, after all. But accept it? That I can't. That I have to say yet again: Okay, I'll play along, I'll look at the clock and wait, and then, afterwards, together, when it's all over, we'll say that I did well and have been good, well done, and then a pat on my head like I'm a dog, because I remained docile, because I didn't whimper, because I didn't bite. Treat. Good girl.

OUTSIDE, BIRDS ARE FLYING. In strange formations or alone. They circle around the trees in the distance and dive down. Some stay behind the Donut's fencing, where they perch momentarily, alone, look around and fly off again. The morning din makes my sleepiness linger. Just now, when the new girl came, I was standing in line with the others: Marissa, Feline, Ashli, Henny, Geraldine, Kyara and Chantal. Soraya left this morning.

Savanna and Marco introduced the new arrival, and that felt weird. I can't remember her name because when they said my name I was seized by a sharp shooting pain in my head that turned everything white and made my ears ring. When I massaged my temples with my hand, I thought *viral meningitis in Burkina Faso*.

The supervisors are drinking coffee. I'm opposite the new girl. She positioned herself close to me as I sat down at the end of the table because I didn't want to talk to anyone. I take it she doesn't either. She's eating with her lank, black hair hanging in front of her face. She brings her sandwich, which she's holding with both hands, in quick movements to her mouth, shoves the bread behind the curtain of her hair and then removes it again when she's chewing. I can't look at it for too long because it makes me feel sick. I don't think that I, when I arrived here, ate so disgustingly. At least she isn't like Henny, whose hair's always hanging in her plate, and which she then has to extract from the mush in her mouth every five minutes. It really almost made me puke once. I wish I was allowed to eat with earplugs in as I sometimes used to do at school. If you wanted to disappear at school, that's something you could just do. Miriam would find it sad if she knew, but the nicest thing was eating my sandwich and reading a book in the loo on the first floor, without all that crap from those posh kids coming my way. Luckily, there are no posh kids here, but despite no longer being 'the new one' I don't exactly fit in either.

All the girls have done stupid things. Most of them can only justify that to themselves by pretending that these things say something about them as a person. The supervisors and Frits play along with this. I did such and such because I'm like this and this. Here the idea persists that if you admit that you've done something wrong and then show remorse because you've had a difficult childhood, or a trauma, or are different from the rest, you will *rehabilitate* better. That's a word I find really ridiculous, rehabilitate. As if there's such a thing as a possibility that you could 'return to a former condition'. That's what it says in the dictionary. Return to a former condition. As if time allows, as if time pauses and will wait for you while you get your shit in order. Time does what it wants and you fight against it.

If you rehabilitate someone it can also mean 'clear someone of a stain he's tainted with'. Fuck that shit. Seriously.

I cast another glance at the girl. She's bent over so far that her fringe is trailing on the table top. Near the tray with stuff for our sandwiches, Marissa sits at the head of the table. She gives me a nod and I nod back. The sunlight dips down through the window and it smells of gym and bread and milk and I suddenly feel really shit. As if I'm about to burst into tears any moment. The headache returns. I quickly push my chair back, bend forward and push my knuckles against the corners of my eyes. Stop it, now, I'm thinking, nothing makes any difference and there's no pain.

'What are you doing?' asks Marco.

'I've got a headache.'

'Drink up your tea.'

'Yeah yeah.' I sit upright again. The girl opposite me looks at me. She has big eyes with long, black lashes, a big, strong nose. She smiles at me and I frown. Then she begins to wolf down her next sandwich.

I want it to be evening. To look out of the window at the stars and not be curious about anything, to be able to say no more than: this is beautiful. Instead, since the shrill beep of my alarm clock this morning I've been finding it difficult to get rid of the lingering feeling from my nightmares. I miss Dad. All those nightmares and the anxious shit oozes into the day with me. I miss Dad more than anyone. That's because I'm sometimes afraid that he'll go while I'm here. Just like Miriam. That she'll go while I'm here, without saying where. That Mum will stay behind, and that when I come home I'll find out that it's my fault and that I can't say it's not. Recently I've been wanting to hear Dad say that everything's okay. That he comes by and says: Everything's okay, I've missed you, everything has been taken care of and it'll be all right. Precisely because it's not all okay and we both know it, and we also know that he'll never be able to take care of anything now.

When I think of my family, I think of very specific moments. Miriam, moving around the neighbourhood, her neck still red from the hand that grabbed her. Mum slowly rising from her desk next to the TV, dragging herself along to the kitchen, her calf muscles tight at every step. Dad, preparing his fishing tackle for the next day and me having to help him. Dad's the sharpest. Throughout, he has his cigarette in his mouth and blows smoke out through his nose. When the smoke drifts past his broad, flat nostrils and he squints a little to make sure that the smoke doesn't prick his eyes, it seems as if he's the only person in the world, the only one of his species, and that we, the rest, are just part of the scenery. At that point he seems far removed from everything that's human. A kind of roving Titan who takes a moment's rest at our dining table before he continues on his quest to find his own kind. A quest that will probably come to nothing. Dad's the only one of his kind.

When Dad's sitting like that, with his fishing tackle, I daren't talk, not even in my mind, even though I want to cut through the tension hanging around him, let him know that I can try to become like him, so that he isn't alone, towering and far away. The moment doesn't pass until Dad puts the cigarette stub in the ashtray on the dining table. By then my hands are clenched and my mouth tastes of the ash in the ashtray.

My mother's an older parent, but my father's lonely and so am I. That's why I can miss him, because I know that he knows what it means to miss someone or something as a lonely person. I see the distance between things, and so does Dad. The distance between him and me is around thirty kilometres and a hundred or so incidents that can't be reversed.

THERE'S A GREEK MYTH in which a guy's damned because he took the gods for a ride. I can't quite remember just now. He's sentenced to life in hell, bound to a mountain to which an enormous eagle flies every day to peck his liver from his body. When the eagle has finished eating the liver, it grows back again overnight and the next day the bird starts all over again. That dude was rescued by Heracles, if I'm right. This is what I'm thinking about when I enter Frits's office.

'Listen,' he says when I sit down. 'I want to make one thing clear.'

'Okay,' I reply.

'I'm not a racist.'

Frits sits back into his chair, hands folded.

'Okay?'

It was Prometheus, the guy who was rescued by Heracles. He gave fire to people because they weren't able to cope with life all that well. Zeus punished him because he shouldn't have done that. He'd been a bad boy. Fire was only meant for the gods. So the gods didn't want us to become smart and skilful, we shouldn't be capable of doing and understanding too much and because one of them felt sorry for us he had to suffer in hell for all eternity.

'So I want this to be clear, I'm not,' he says. 'And I understand why you distrust me, but I'm here for you and hope that you'll be able to see this as we carry on with our meetings.'

I'm thinking of Prometheus because I'm imagining him, like in a cartoon, as the one who was holding the light bulb above our heads when we were groping in the dark.

'I've no choice, have I?' I say as Frits opens my file.

I wonder what Prometheus thought when he was free of that eagle, no longer in hell. I wonder if he'd do it again, if he'd liberate us again from cluelessness. If he'd look at Frits and think: This man needs a light bulb above his head.

'I've got an idea,' I say, 'about why you took part in that programme. And that makes me angry.'

'Why does it make you angry?' Frits asks.

'Because you pretend you know something you don't actually know.'

'And what do I not know?'

This is what he does not know: Prometheus pulls the cord, his long arm reaching downwards from wherever it is he is now, and all of a sudden *ping*, light above Frits's stupid head.

'Do you know the Narcissus myth?' I ask.

'Narcissus?' Frits is wearing a T-shirt saying ROUTE 66. For a while, and I know exactly at which point I began to notice it, everyone at school started to wear shirts with lettering. ROUTE 66, SUMMERTIME IN HAWAII, 77 in huge numbers, SCAPA SPORTS, DE PUTA MADRE, VON DUTCH, FEMALE BODY INSPECTOR in curly Coca-Cola letters, ROUTE 69, ROUTE 67, ROUTE 95, ARIZONA STATE.

'Narcissus, who was fantastically good-looking, gazed down into holy water during the time of the Greeks,' I tell him, 'and he saw his own reflection, crystal clear. They didn't have mirrors during that time, I think. He fell in love with his own reflection.'

At some point the shirts were no longer in fashion. At some point people stopped wearing shirts with American routes on them and girls began to wear fancy body warmers, boys sweaters with brand names on them. G-STAR RAW DENIM, PRADA SPORTS, DIESEL. Frits's T-shirt is washed-out. It's become pale yellow, with a grey undertone. The route's discoloured, and where the letters were there's still some sort of sheen in places, but the numbers are dull.

'He fell in love with his own reflection,' I say, 'but you can't kiss your reflection, or talk to it, or marry it. It made him sad and he died.'

'Yeah, okay,' said Frits.

'He didn't know he was seeing himself,' I say.

'What has this got to do with me?'

'Narcissism's derived from—'

'Yes, I get that,' he throws in quickly.

'All I mean to say,' I say, and I'm not looking at Frits, I'm looking outside, at the blades of grass that are tender and green, that move along with the wind, 'is that you don't know how you come across to me.'

'I don't think that's the lesson you learn from this story.'

'No, right,' I reply. 'But I always wonder what it would've been like if Narcissus had known what he looked like. Bending over that water, obsessed by himself.'

The image in *Hello Jungle* in which Frits is standing next to a farmer in his yard. The farmer's called Bassa. He's tiny, skinny. He reaches as far as Frits's shoulder. Hours from the big city, surrounded by chickens and cows and goats, and Frits is looking directly into the lens and bellows, 'Come on, it's crazy, it's mad, isn't it, it isn't *normal*, is it? No shower, no phone connection, no electricity.' Next to him stands a girl my age, one of the chief's daughters, stripped to the waist, the shell strings above her breasts, her non-comprehending gaze focussed on Frits, the bucket of feed in her hand, dangling next to her calf. What kind of image is that? Has he watched it again himself? Almost a year ago he was on TV. My father was dozing with his mouth open, the remote control in his hand. He began to snore while I was watching Frits. My mother was sitting at the PC, with her back to the TV, in the office chair that's normally in the corner by the bookcase. Where was Miriam?

'A lot of people really enjoyed watching it,' says Frits, and in my mind's eye I still see the enormous posters of Bassa in traditional outfit in shopfront windows, the cut-price DVDs in a crate.

'I must say that the final edit was a bit off.'

'Me too,' I say. 'Not exactly a friendly reflection.'

'I'm pleased to hear that,' he says, and he laughs, short, yellow teeth.

I open my mouth to explain what I really mean, but a sparrow flies slap bang into the window. He crashes down on the paving stones outside and begins to convulse. Frits also glances at the scene. He looks searchingly. I wonder if Frits is the kind of person who, when he's having a walk in the park and a sparrow's dying, will leave it there. That he'll think, that's nature. Perhaps he tramples it to death.

The sparrow chirps briefly and then there's silence. Its little beak's at a funny angle, its wings don't move. I hope it's dead, not paralysed and quietly dying a miserable death that we can't see.

The eagle that ate Prometheus's liver every day, what did it do when Prometheus was liberated? What did it eat every day?

'It'll be horribly smelly if we don't clear it up,' says Frits with a pained expression. 'Poor creature.'

'Yes,' I say, but I don't get up, and neither does Frits.

I can't take it. The image must go. Frits's and his girlfriend's laughter, when the welcome dance is being performed, then Frits trying to kill a chicken, then Frits putting ochre clay onto one of the women, a ritual. The chief shouts that he isn't allowed to do that. *No no no no!* he shouts, waving his arms. The way Frits slides his hands along her back, making her jump when she turns around, as she thought it was his girlfriend who was rubbing her with the clay. *No no no no!* The way he laughs, again, the way his girlfriend laughs, again, the way she asks whether he's enjoying it.

Dirty sod, his girlfriend calls him.

The girl asks him, with subtitles, whether Frits's wife has a mobile phone, whether she can take pictures with it. No one translates her question. All people who're groping in the dark with no one to give them light.

Frits turns to me again.

'Can you and I try to get on with each other in a normal way?'

'Yes,' I say.

I think I say that because our old childminder comes to mind, Kaat. Kaat is sixty now, she's a grandmother, she looked after us three times a week when Mum and Dad had to work late; Dad in the furniture factory and Mum at the office about which I never know exactly what she does there. Kaat and her big, gold crucifix in her living room, and Jesus painted in white and red and brown, suspended from the gold. Kaat and her parakeet, in a

61

cage in the kitchen. Kaat who lowered her shutters after six p.m. because 'no one needs to see what there is to steal here', and every week when the asylum seeker centre came to the village, accompanied a group of women and children on foot to go to mass in the church where Miriam and I were baptised. Kaat would swear sometimes, when she listened to the radio, at 'all those sodding foreigners who come and mess things up here'. She could do both, and the link between the two things may've been obscured in the dark, in the not understanding why the water ripples when you want to give it a kiss.

'Everyone does something they regret at some point in their lives,' says Frits.

'That's why,' I say.

'What matters is that your intentions are good, that when things go wrong you can account for that, that you can control yourself when things get out of hand.' It's as if he's saying it to himself.

Frits's girlfriend who pukes after having a bowl of food shoved into her hand. Frits who gags, who casts a meaningful glance at the lens and shows the contents of his bowl. The cameraman filming a farmer who laughs, with his hands on his knees, when Frits tries to catch a chicken, but the critter keeps escaping. Goddammit that shitty animal.

'It's *authentic*,' said Frits. They are quite sweet people, really. Look, sunset. They aren't like us. They experience life *differently*. A *mirror* is held in front of your face, what a cushy life we have, when you see this.

'Life doesn't always feel fair. So I can understand that you're angry,' he says to me now, to himself.

'No, you're different,' says Kaat when Miriam asked her one Wednesday afternoon whether we were also bloody blacks.

The structures, Aunt Céleste said, are turned against you.

'Exciting,' said the man who went to the Amazon with his wife and two children, drums beating and whooping in the background, 'and a bit, well, what do you call it . . .?'

The enormous Xingu River. The serious look on the men's faces as they were cleaning the fish on the riverbank.

'What do you call it . . .? Scary. Yes, quite scary as well. You really don't know what's in store. They are and will continue to be primitive troglodytes.'

And then he came into shot. Or at any rate I saw a man with a ponytail sitting in a black office chair, behind him a cross-trainer with clothes draped over it. What was it that Frits said? The savannah, dry grass, broad tree branches and the setting sun, as if we were watching *The Lion King*. And then that ponytail, that chair.

'Above all I hope we can learn from each other,' he said.

They were wearing bright red robes. The women, children on their hips, trudging towards a well. Primitive. So the word's just a word, but the word's also the deepest image of that word. He hasn't invented that image, he just whispers it at his reflection.

Frits packing his bag.

Frits and his girlfriend, laughing, saying goodbye to their family, who, in the car to the airport, wonder where they will sleep, whether they have showers, what they're going to do all day.

'That's the result of colonialism and patriarchy,' said Aunt Céleste, clutching a bottle of beer in the webcam, from her new apartment in Barcelona.

Time works in strange ways. Sometimes the things you experience seem to be totally unrelated, and sometimes time seems to stop so that all of a sudden you can see how everything, with all the wafer-thin lines in between, is connected. So that you can *understand* it. Sometimes time asks for action.

I say: 'I'm often angry as well, yes.'

I don't say what Aunt Céleste said, with her beer bottle, her jewellery.

I don't say what Kaat said, with her shutters down, her hands fluffing up the cushions on her sofa: 'You guys are just Dutch.'

'How do you feel today?' Frits then asks.

'Tired,' I reply.

'How was your week?'

'Tiring.'

'Why tiring?'

'Because I've been doing a lot of thinking.'

'About what?'

'Myself.' I look at the sparrow that's probably dead and at Frits, the man from the TV, in his seat. 'My family, home, you.'

'I can imagine,' he says, 'that you're worrying a bit and that that requires energy.'

'It's more,' I say, 'that I'm thinking about how they're worrying. And I miss them. And I'm thinking about school. About the subjects I'm not getting here.'

'Do you miss school?'

'The subjects, yes,' I say.

Frits writes and I look out of the window, the glass that's really a wall.

'What subject do you miss most?' Frits asks.

'Dutch,' I say.

'You read a lot, don't you?'

'Yes.'

'What have you read recently?'

And so it carries on for a bit longer. I talk and talk, and slowly I forget the images, along with the feeling from my nightmares; they drain into space, out of the building, for now.

IT'S NOT AS IF HE said something unspeakable. It's not as if, like the other people who were in the Amazon, all he did was swear and say that it was filthy, filthy filthy filthy. It's not as if, like Kaat, he said that Dad didn't really deserve to get ill, but that that short fuse of his didn't really help either.

They're different over there, there's no denying that, she said.

They're different over here, there's no denying that, he said.

It's not as if he mimicked the village elder, like the boy from Zutphen in Kenya, who snatched the stick from the old man and began to brag as if he was drunk. The old man asked if he was suffering from sunstroke. No, said the boy, you are with your mumbo jumbo. Laughter all around. But not from Frits.

You mustn't think that you're alone, Miriam once said.

I really mustn't make any links between those images.

The way it was always the same two boys, Paul and Salvatore, who came looking for me at break time and sometimes found me, and then the same thing happened as in the Amazon in Kenya in Namibia. The light isn't on. No one brought it. What happens in the dark's boring, tedious.

I'm mimicking you, Salvatore laughed as he swaggered around the chemistry lab like a gorilla.

With your mumbo jumbo. Laughter all around.

You mustn't think that you're alone, Miriam once said. You mustn't think that other people don't have a hard time either, or aren't sad, that that shit doesn't happen to others as well.

The way it was such a cliché. So cheap.

We all have a fucking hard time, Salomé, Miriam said, leaning against the garage wall, watching me hit the punchball with my fist after school. We all have a fucking hard time. It's not just about how *you* feel the whole time. That's what she said.

65

WHAT I HATE ABOUT the cleaning duties is that they shove a mop and a cleaning rag into your hand and then leave you to it, knowing full well that they'll have to come back after fifteen minutes to put an end to all the bullshit with a load of threats. Especially when you have to clean with Ashli who's always got something to say about 'foreigners'. Meaning me. And Marissa. And Zainab, therefore. That's what the new girl's called. She hardly talks, even when you ask her a direct question, which is something Ashli does all the time. Shitty questions I'd have whacked her for a long time ago.

'So do you live with eight family members in a flat or something, like all those Turkish people in the North End?' Ashli asks, flinging her yellow cleaning cloth against the wall of one of the showers. Zainab's scrubbing the floor on her knees and I try not to look at her long hair skimming the soapy water half the time. I have to clean the loos, but they're completely covered in piss and shit, because clearly no one picks up how to leave a loo in a decent state after crapping here. So I do the walls of the showers first, as Ashli always starts whinging when she has to remove hair from the drains.

'Hello?' she calls to Zainab. 'Can we talk? Or do you not speak any Dutch either?'

Zainab shuffles backwards, towards the next shower cubicle, and keeps her mouth shut.

'Or can you only speak Turkish? What are you really anyway?'

'Why don't you just shut your gob and clean the sinks,' I say, and Ashli goes over to the cleaning cloth she splashed against the walls and aims for the bucket. She misses and the filthy water splatters against my shoes and lower legs.

'Did I ask you something?'

'Just clean those sinks,' I say, wringing out my own cloth. Zainab looks up from underneath her fringe and I try to pull a just-leave-it face.

'Fucking lesbo,' says Ashli.

'You should keep your gob shut, Ashli.'

'When I'm out of here, I'll find you, my boyfriend will totally kill you.'

I have to laugh. And Zainab also chuckles. Ashli pulls a face and flips her ugly highlights over her shoulder.

'What? Do you think he won't beat you up?'

'Doesn't interest me,' I say, and I carry on with the next shower. Zainab continues scrubbing, but over the edge of the partition wall between the two showers I see how Ashli goes over to the bucket, gets her cloth and of course, because why not, hurls it straight at Zainab's back. A dirty, wet throw. Zainab stops scrubbing, gets up and the cloth splashes off her back onto the floor.

'I'll tear all your fucking insides out,' she says softly.

I long to be somewhere else instead of bang in the middle of this kind of bollocks that isn't worth my attention. I move backwards when Ashli comes running for Zainab, and before what happens happens I leave the bathroom and go and wait in the corridor. There's screaming and I see how Marco comes running.

'What's going on here?' he calls. I take a step to the side and carry on leftwards, to my room, because I don't fancy this. I go and stand in front of my wall and stare at it, to stop the boiling inside me.

In therapy Frits said that I should think about what I want to learn during this period. A goal to aim for. If you have a kind of higher goal you can make all pain functional. The end justifies the means, as it were. Then pain's a marker on the road you travelled. It's a way of looking at it, true. Pain as a learning moment, something to get around with all your cleverness, to use as an emblem of everything you have left behind. Or pain as proof: This is what it cost, what I achieved. You have improved yourself, haven't you? And as a reward you'll never have to suffer again. We're all going to give you a big round of applause, we're so glad you've done well! I said to Frits that more than anything I wanted peace. I said that it felt as if I was lost in a forest, now. No birds are singing and I can hear no water splashing, nothing. I can't get my bearings. I don't know where I'm going and what I'm doing here.

Marco enters my room and I turn towards him.

'And what are you doing here?'

'You don't want me to get involved in all that now, do you?' I say. He puts his hands on his hips.

'Yes,' he fumes. 'And now finish your tasks, or I'll report you.'

'Are you getting angry with me when they start having a scrap?' I turn away and skirt past him to leave the room. He grabs me by the arm. I feel the thunderstorm roll so loudly in my head that I don't know what I said to him, standing on my toes, my nose almost touching his, my hand on top of his, which is squeezing my other arm, but he immediately lets go. He doesn't say anything. Nor do I. And it's only now that I hear the real rain, outside, tapping against the window. And it's only now that I feel that it's cold inside, the draught around my ankles.

'Sorry?' Marco says softly.

'I'm on my way,' I say.

'What did you say?'

'Nothing,' I say. 'I'm sorry.' Then I return to the bathroom, fast, shaking. Marco follows me suspiciously and watches me pick up the cleaning things I left behind. Ashli has gone. Zainab's cleaning the loo. Her hair's in a mess and she doesn't lift her head to look at me. I slowly walk past her and start on the basins.

'And now no more messing about.'

When Marco has left we clean in silence for a while. Ashli doesn't return.

'Did you win?' I then ask. I hear the cleaning brush that Zainab's scrubbing against the porcelain fall silent.

'Undecided,' she says.

I WAS EIGHT WHEN AUNT CÉLESTE came to stay. She and my uncle Honoré are Dad's only family members ever to have flown to the Netherlands to visit us. They were still married at the time. They stayed for three weeks. It was summer and it only rained once or twice, I think, during the time that they were there. We sat outside all the time in fact, in our small back garden. I slept with Miriam, in the attic, so that my uncle and aunt could sleep in my room with my cousin Antoine. Antoine in my single bed and Uncle and Aunt on an air mattress. Mum spent the whole weekend cleaning the house for their visit, every room had to be spic and span. Dad was sulking because Uncle Honoré had a well-paid job in Yaoundé and had built an enormous house on the compound where they'd grown up.

'So,' he said, 'I know what he'll say when he sees this house.'

One of the days that they were staying with us Aunt Céleste climbed up to the attic where I was reading, I think. Although I don't have clear memories of those three weeks, I think I was there because I was shy, wanted to be alone.

I was sitting on the edge of the bed I was sharing with Miriam, and Aunt Céleste knocked on the open door.

'Here you are,' she said, standing in the doorway, hands on her hips. I can well remember how caught out I felt. Aunt Céleste sat down next to me.

'What are you doing?'

'Reading.'

'All on your own, here upstairs?'

I put my book aside, pushed the hair back from my face. As if it only just struck her then, she grasped for my curls with her hand.

'My God,' she said with an exaggerated sigh. A shock went through my body, which I'm still feeling now. I think I found her

69

disrespectful. Because Mum had given up trying to find a hair-dresser in the area who could give my hair a decent cut, Dad did it, if he could get me to sit down for it, in the garage. Dad cut his own hair, using three table mirrors he placed around himself in order to get an overview of all parts of his head. It never went beyond a round Afro cut, but it always looked neat. Miriam had looser curls, which allowed a wide comb to slide through easily when she'd just washed her hair. Mine was frizzy and grew quickly. When Dad had tackled it, I'd usually walk around with a kind of Bernie Mac-ish Afro like a mini-version of him, until it grew out and I could gather it in a small ponytail. When Dad had cut my hair my primary school teacher always called me Little Black Pete.

Miriam always had pigtails. And a bun. When she wore her hair loose and had rubbed coconut oil in it, it would dance around.

I don't know why Dad hadn't given me a cut before Uncle and Aunt came to stay. I do know that as soon as they arrived I felt that Aunt Céleste disapproved of my appearance.

A moment later I was sitting on the bed with tears in my eyes, staring at the cupboard on the other side of Miriam's attic room. Aunt Céleste hurt me. I sat with clenched fists in my lap, fighting off the tears, as she was pulling my hair. She'd drawn two lines over my skull using a fine comb with a long pin, from the middle of my forehead to my neck and from my right to my left temple, to divide my hair into four sections. Two of those sections had already been crammed into tight plaits. She was working on the third, the one on the left below, where the hairs at the nape of my neck were burning as Aunt Céleste was working them into the plait. It was the first time in my life that I'd seen her in the flesh. I'd looked at the photos of my father's family, in the hall next to the front door. Big portraits of people dressed in colour-ful clothes, women with shining hair, long braids, or reddish wigs and heavy eye make-up. They all had full lips, with dark brown lipstick and polished nails. None of the women had my round-cut Afro hair. The men in black suits and leather loafers had adopted serious poses. The girls, my cousins, wore the same outfits as I was wearing that afternoon, powder-coloured, white, blue, pink lace, their hair in plaits and ponytails. The male cousins in white short-sleeved shirts and bow ties. Mum called it Sunday best, Dad called it smart.

It was terrible, that afternoon, because in the photo, in my dreams, Aunt Céleste had looked like a princess. In her and Uncle Honoré's wedding portrait she was wearing a white cocktail dress and heavy make-up. She didn't smile, gazed into the distance next to my tall uncle with his moustache and golden ring. She *really* looked like a princess, serious and light. But in the attic, when she was doing my hair, she laughed the whole time. She ruined the fantasies I'd had about her, based on the things my father had told us about her: how nice she was, a quiet student, an intelligent girl, good cook. So I thought she was a kind of black Cinderella made of little stars and glass, with pale blue dresses, chic, who moved like a ballerina. But Aunt Céleste was no Cinderella. She didn't flitter. She smelled spicy and warm, not like the ballerina in my head, and she gesticulated a lot when she was speaking. When she smiled you could see the golden crown at the back of her mouth, the dark gums stretching over her white teeth. And she chatted as if I was her best friend.

'You've got exactly the same hair as my friend Anja,' she said, rubbing oil into my hair that she'd gone downstairs to get, '*très sec*. Incredible. We sometimes put pure honey in it to make it less dull. You should really come into town with me, we can go and look for a shop that sells jojoba. All those white people shampoos don't work for your hair.' She got going on a new braid, and my head flopped to the side. I gave her an angry look.

'And those flakes. Get some avocado, bit of yoghurt. Keep it in for fifteen minutes.'

'I'm allergic to yoghurt,' I said in my best French. She looked at me briefly and laughed.

'Not to eat!'

Her summer skirts, her grumbling about the weather, her gold earrings, the diamond on her wedding ring that would bump against my head every so often when she pulled the comb through my hair. Her hands kept on moving, she talked nonstop and loudly. The skin of her arms glowed. I hated the fact that she'd mix French and Ewondo at times and that I then wouldn't be able to follow her. She scared me with her enormous energy, low voice and incomprehensible words, her strange 'r's, and then those hands that had groped for my head without asking and decided they had to do something to my hair.

'Come on, little Salomé,' she said, pulling my hair again as I tried to release my head. 'Don't be such a nuisance. We're nearly done. Then you can go and play.' She found it normal that she could hurt me.

'It'll be a surprise for your mum and your sister,' she said. *Une surprise.*

Très sec.

As I remember it, I was sweating until the sweat trickled into the backs of my knees and my eczema began to sting.

When we were ready she walked me downstairs holding me by the hand. She'd put white ribbon bows in my hair. My family's ohs and ahs. Miriam and Antoine stopped playing on the floor of the living room, and Miriam looked aghast at my hair. Uncle Honoré called me a *vraie dame*, and Aunt Céleste made me turn around so that everyone could have a good look. When I threw a glance at Miriam again, she returned it with a furious gaze.

'What do you think about it yourself?' Mum asked, inspecting me.

'*Je m'en fous,*' I said, as I had heard Dad say so often on the telephone. 'Can I carry on reading now?'

Silence. Then Aunt Céleste's loud laughter. Uncle Honoré and Dad gave me a shocked look. Dad came over to me and tapped me softly on the back of my burning head. Mum bit her lower lip. 'You go,' she said, and waved me off.

When all that terrible attention had passed I went to the loo and lowered the lid so that I could stand on it and look at myself in the mirror above the basin. I gave myself a miserable stare in return. Four worms of hair shot up from my head, the bows were ridiculous. *Une vraie dame.* She had picked the wrong kid to use as a dummy.

When Aunt Céleste and Uncle Honoré left that summer, she cried. She hugged me for a long time and said that I was special. Miriam also cried. I think out of jealousy. I waited until Aunt Céleste was ready.

It's not just all about how *you* feel, Miriam said in the garage.

Antoine had clasped his arms around Uncle Honoré's leg and didn't cry, he looked on.

'Such a special girl, so exceptional, so clever,' Aunt Céleste said, and she lowered herself onto her knees to give me another hug, at eye level this time. She smelled of spicy perfume. She was clutching a new bag, bought in Tilburg. In Tilburg she'd also bought jars with hair products for Miriam and me from a Hindustani shop.

Every day Aunt Céleste had fiddled with my hair. She explained how she did it. Which comb, which oil, what kind of elastic. Bookworms should also do something about their appearance, she said.

This day, too, the last one, I stood waiting with a burning skull until she'd finally be gone and I'd be able to undo those plaits. Miriam's head was glowing with grease. All on her own she'd managed to oil her curls, comb a tight ponytail backwards. Her baby hair stuck in small shiny wavelets against her forehead.

'I'll call you,' Aunt Céleste cried.

When, later that day, Dad combed out my braids, he was very careful. When I doubled up or hissed between my teeth because he pulled a sensitive hair, he stopped immediately and blew on my forehead.

'Your aunt's right,' he said. I scratched my eczema and he tapped my hand. 'Don't, Salomé.' He blew on it. His voice close to my ears while he was combing.

'Your aunt's right. You are special,' he teased. 'You watch out.'

I DON'T THINK I'M SPECIAL. Or at any rate not in the way that Dad and Aunt Céleste meant. I'm not special. I'm just a sourpuss. I like being alone. I used to work hard. I didn't moan. *Très sec.*

Here, nothing interesting happens to talk about, nothing special. There's only a constant, yucky, dragging feeling. The kind of feeling you get when you see slugs slither towards a leaf in your garden. The concentration. Going on and on. Meanwhile vehicles whizz past: cars, mopeds and even bicycles in the distance. It's barely visible, but if you look closely you see that vibrations create tracks in the slime.

I try to keep things tolerable with books. With smoking cigarettes next to Marissa in the recreation yard. With film evenings. With the few scuffles a month when weed's found in someone's room, a boyfriend doesn't turn up during visiting time, or one of the kids runs away during temporary release only to be found again. Sometimes we hear boys scream, when the windows of their units are open. There's a lot more fighting going on over there than here. We are besieged by tension. It quivers and buzzes and becomes thick and enormous and palpable. Then it bursts; after that it becomes normal again.

The rules that apply here are based on sad things, I think, things that have been broken, things you don't want to know about, very slow, quivering slime, as sluggish as that. Not on the feeling that you're special. Not that that's good. They'd rather have no honey, no jojoba. They prefer *très sec.*

When your hair becomes too dry it breaks off.

It's the slowness and then the outbursts and the fact that no one bats an eyelid. It's part of the images that keep coming back in my mind. It's the constant threat of an explosion, but when it arrives, it's ignored. It's a very deep focus from which I keep expecting that if I go along with it, we'll arrive somewhere. But usually this isn't the case. It doesn't end. Everyone carries on regardless.

It's as if I'm exposed to something dark. It hangs over all of us and connects us, but is different for everyone. It's as if we're all in our own vortex: we're moving, but aren't going anywhere.

Or maybe it's not a vortex. Maybe it's a pit, we all have our own pit we've fallen into. No one wants to accept how far down they've ended up.

MY THOUGHTS ARE OLD. They repeat themselves in strange formations, like the birds that fly over the building, like the memories that thrust themselves upon me.

Me playing outside with Sammie and Bartje from my class and secondary school boys coming to bully us, challenging us, trampling wooden forts, that's what I'm thinking about.

Once I got angry with a boy from the technical college and when I kicked him, he booted me with full force, in my stomach. The pain made me cry.

'Wait,' said his friend, 'isn't that a girl?'

Une vraie dame, Uncle Honoré said.

That looks smart, said Dad when he forced me to wear a dress when Uncle and Aunt came to stay.

When I played a game of football with the boys and no one in the game knew I was a girl, I had to suffer like the boys. When you fall over, there's laughter. No one to blow on your graze.

I wasn't special. I did once ask Aunt Céleste on MSN, when Miriam wasn't there. What made me so special?

'You're one of those children,' she said, 'who do things in their own way, don't accept the rules of the world without questioning them.'

She said it as a compliment.

She came to the attic to do my hair because I had to look normal.

The black man with the down coat in the summer. Zainab scrubbing the bathroom floor. Aunt Céleste with her beer and her webcam, the jojoba oil. Dad spooling thread around his fishing reel. Miriam with her snapped cigarettes. In court, Paul's lawyer pronounced my name wrongly. I rose to my feet and said 'never'. These images don't follow in a logical sequence. Events don't either. Nothing regenerates, it doesn't get lighter. No light bulb above my head. The eagle returns every day to pick at my liver. Thinking is slow and I'm constantly interrupted: homework, therapy, dinner, chores, keeping your head down and then being able to make a phone call and you should be pleased with that, and you are, but what is it then, what are you going on about? What more do you want? everything here seems to asks me. Just work hard, don't ask why, just do it, don't moan.

WE'RE HAVING A PHONE CALL. Dad, Mum, Miriam and me. Like we do almost every day we're speaking on the phone, and I try to concentrate on how they say things, I want to be able to preserve their voices somewhere.

'Miriam's studying for her final exams. Work's on a roll for me. Dad's been given new medication,' says Mum.

'Oh, and is it working?'

'Yes,' says Dad.

'He's lost his appetite,' says Miriam, and then there's silence.

'That's not nice.'

'No,' says Dad.

'Aunt Céleste's sent you a letter. We haven't opened it. I'll bring it along when I next visit,' says Mum.

'Do you think I'll be able to understand it when I read it?'

'I've bought a French–Dutch dictionary. I'll bring that too. Then you can look up words you don't understand. How are things over there?'

'Are you still getting therapy from that dude from the TV?' Miriam asks.

'Yes,' I say.

'Is he still revolting?'

'Well . . .' I say.

'You'll get through it,' says Mum.

'I hope so. It's boring here. But the sun's shining. There's a new girl. She's called Zainab. She's quite nice.'

'Hang on in there!' says Dad. He sounds upset. I hear some murmuring, but I can't hear what they're saying. It's as if Mum and Dad are whispering to each other. Miriam coughs. She sniffs long and audibly.

'Carlita's giving birth in a week. Her mother's back from Suriname to be there for it.'

'It's going to be a boy, right?'

'No, a girl.'

'Will you still be living at home when I come back?'

'Don't know.'

'Listen, Salomé, it's important that you do your best in the therapy sessions,' says Mum.

'I'm doing my best. Really.'

'Yeah yeah,' says Miriam.

'I've just finished *The Stranger*, by the way.'

'What did you think of it?' Mum asks.

'I think I liked it, but maybe I don't quite get it. They were beautiful images. Especially of the sun.'

'Well, that's perfectly okay, isn't it, that you thought the images were beautiful?'

'How long does Dad need to take those pills?'

'As long as it's necessary,' he says. 'They make you ill, but that's the idea.'

'Even more ill,' says Miriam.

'Tell me something,' I say. 'Just any old thing.'

Mum talks about her work, that a colleague got so drunk during an office party that he fell asleep on the loo. This makes Miriam laugh. I also pretend I'm laughing, and after that Dad talks about an oven dish he'd made on Sunday that he'd ruined. Miriam says it was quite nice, Mum too, but he says that he only managed to polish off less than half his plate. Then all three fall silent again. My father who can't eat.

During Classical Studies we were shown lots of photos of Greek statues, all those athletes and such, all those fully trained bodies, thighs on which you could almost see the veins, the awkward poses that seemed to make their abs contract. I imagine one of these statues gradually being hacked out until it's no more than a skinny little man on a plinth. My father once I'm home. The marble no longer creamy white but dirty grey. The ancient bronze that's gone green all over. Mrs Doormans, with her remote in her right hand in order to project the slides onto the classroom's white wall, who explained that that's called patina. Verdigris. It's caused by rain or oxidation. When your body's wasted away by cancer you form a patina layer, that's how I imagine it with those pills. That when I'm back, Dad will be covered in green scabs, his interior acidic as a result of all the juices in his body having got out of balance thanks to the cells that are killing him. He doesn't eat and so has no way of keeping himself in good shape.

'Are you still there?' Mum asks.

'Yes,' I say.

'It's good to talk to you,' she says.

'They've given that dude a glass eye, by the way,' says Miriam, and then Dad gives her an earful and Mum sighs deeply into the receiver, and then Mum says, 'I thought we'd agreed that—' but she put her hand over the receiver and I can't hear it. Miriam's gone, I think.

'Hello?'

'It'll all be all right,' says Mum.

'Okay,' I say. 'What did she say?'

'Just hang on in there.'

Dad has fallen silent.

'Who has a glass eye?' I ask.

'Salomé.'

'Who? Paul?'

'Yes,' Mum says softly, 'Paul. But you shouldn't worry about that.'

'And Salvatore?'

'I don't know. We've stopped shopping in the village.'

'Why? Why's that?'

I want to talk more about it. I want to know everything. But Mum begins about the car having to go to the garage, a scratch on the door, et cetera. I listen without responding until our time's up. Then she says bye, I love you, keep going, till Friday, don't do anything stupid so that we can't come and see you again. I say yes, me too me too me too, till then. I go to my room and lie down on the bed and think about yoghurt, honey, oil, eye gloop, all shit that seeps through your fingers.

THE SUMMER AFTER AUNT CÉLESTE and Uncle Honoré had stayed with us, we went to Cameroon. Uncle Honoré had had business dealings in Brussels or Paris or some other city in Belgium or France and had been to see us a few times by train. He kept harping on at Dad that we should come.

'Your children don't understand the culture,' he said during one of those visits. 'They hardly understand any French, only baby talk.' He sat at the table shaking his head. Mum had made something complicated with lamb, but he only prodded his food.

'They're children,' Dad said. 'What do you expect?'

Miriam chuckled, but Dad tapped her on the hand and her fork clanked onto the table. After dinner they drank cognac. I heard Uncle Honoré try to convince Mum.

'It's important,' he said, 'that your children get to know their Cameroonian side. The French language. They know your side, and that's fine, that's good. But Samuel owes it to them.'

He then turned to Dad.

'And Céleste would like to see the children again.'

Later, via a courier service, Uncle Honoré sent us a CD-ROM with an English-language programme for learning French. By playing games, puzzles, rebuses, conversation games with cartoon figures, you increased your vocabulary, made sentences. Miriam enjoyed it. I usually sat next to her on a chair when she was playing it. Dad and Mum saved up all year for the tickets and we went during the summer holidays.

The flight was long and tiring. Mum found it exciting. I held her hand throughout and couldn't eat. I was scared. I was sweating. I'd never flown before. Miriam hadn't either, but she simply wasn't scared of anything. She didn't think about anything, she just did things and then it would turn out all right. We changed planes in Istanbul and I followed close on Mum's heels through the airport's terminals. The queues, the ads. I felt sick the whole time and it only got worse when we got on the plane to Douala. The screaming, the uniforms, the screeching babies, the air that smelled of hundreds of different people's breath. When we arrived at the airport another uncle picked us up, Jacques. He looked like a younger, but sterner version of Dad, and he walked extremely upright, as if he was in the army. In the car they spoke French and Ewondo with each other. Uncle Jacques more Ewondo, but the further we drove into town the less French Dad talked and the more he rolled his 'r's and made a singing 'z' with his tongue. I fell asleep against Mum, who was sitting in the middle of the back seat with me on one side and Miriam on the other. Miriam looked out of the window; I kept waking up with a start and dropping off again. The unknown smells made me dream about caves and kidnappings, drowning. The city was strangling me, that's what it felt like, and the dust on the big motorway looked as if it would actually suffocate me. And then, when we had finally escaped the city, passing tall trees and bushes along the long, bumpy road, we followed the tarmac past the shanty towns and villages, via a long, untarmacked road straight onto my family's compound. I'd first expected to see a lot of fields with crops, like in our village back home, and cows grazing behind fences before, in the distance, there'd be a gate or an enormous barn. But instead, all of a sudden a tall, white building with narrow windows and a big veranda rose up with two cars parked in front, their tyres brown from the dust. The trees around the compound were huge. One grew over the house and provided shelter over the veranda. Behind the house, the estate. Insects everywhere. The soil was red; my aunts, who were waiting for us outside the door, were wearing coloured shirts, polo shirts. Aunt Céleste up front, with an older woman who looked like her, and waved at me and laughed when Uncle Jacques stopped the car.

Reluctantly I crawled out of the car, and Aunt Céleste immediately pulled me towards her to greet me.

'My little Salomé!' she exclaimed. I allowed myself to be kissed, allowed hands with golden rings or silver rings or no rings at all to tug my hair, squeeze my cheeks.

'My God, my God,' Aunt Céleste called, tugging the long plait Mum had been able to put in my hair after a great deal of toing and froing. I looked at Mum, who blushed. Positioned amid the suitcases next to the car, she was sweating, kissing aunts and greeting uncles. She didn't come to my rescue. Miriam was talking French with our cousins.

'And how are you?' an older aunt asked, placing her big hand on my cheek and bending over.

'Fine,' I said. Silence. Dad came and stood next to me, lifted his foot to encourage me, the tip of his shoe pressing against my leg.

'*Comment ça va . . .*' Dad started.

'*Avec vous,*' I mumbled.

'She looks just like you,' the aunt with the low voice said when she stood upright again.

We went inside. Dad disappeared with his brothers via the back door to inspect the estate. I stayed inside with Miriam and the aunts. Aunt Céleste wanted to show us the house Uncle Honoré had built. She dragged us from room to room, some spaces dark due to the dimming curtains. I was hot. Everything was clammy. Mum panted as she climbed the stairs. Miriam and an unfamiliar cousin were both running along the corridors. Here was the bathroom. The generator's behind the house, yes. Here the guest room for the children. Keep all the windows closed otherwise it'll get damp and hot.

Dinner came hours later. We ate something with peanuts and a spicy sauce around the big dining table, around the coffee table in the sitting area. Everyone was present, and sat where they could. There was music, the TV was on, Antoine screamed when his cartoon was interrupted for the news. Dishes were passed around over my head while I ate rice as closely huddled up to Mum as possible.

'She's very shy, isn't she?' an old aunt with a slow, creaking voice asked. She had a small yellow cloth tied in her hair. I couldn't stop looking at her mouth, how she slowly ate fish and long beans, chewing carefully around the gap of her missing lower teeth. She reminded me of Grandma, how she shuffled through the house in Breskens in the mornings without her false teeth. 'Or can she not talk?'

'That's what we sometimes wonder,' replied Dad. Ha ha ha. Miriam threw me a grin from the other side of the table.

When everyone went home it was dark, I was kissed, my cheek squeezed. The goodbyes took a long time. I wanted to be with Mum, she was still talking animatedly.

I slept badly next to Miriam that night, in the spare room in a bed that was fractionally too small. I saw it getting increasingly light behind the curtains; I only dropped off in the blue, bright morning light and while I was drifting off I hoped I'd wake up in the Netherlands. I hoped it would rain.

I WOKE UP AND IT was quiet in the house. Miriam had already got up, her blankets were lying folded back on her bed. No screaming children, no radio or TV sounds. No smell from the food that was usually being prepared throughout the day. It was so still that I got the feeling that I'd been left behind. I slipped straight from the bed into my slippers and opened the spare room's wooden door. I called hello. Nothing. I slowly went down the stairs and saw Aunt Céleste sitting in the living room. She was asleep in her chair, in front of the TV, which was on mute. I went over to her and placed my hand on her leg. She woke with a start and instantly began to smile.

'Finally awake? Come, come.' She lifted me up and carried me, with my head on her shoulder, through the house to the veranda. A small table stood next to the plastic chair I was told to sit in. She disappeared inside and came back with tea and fruit. Aunt Céleste sat down in the seat next to me. I drank and ate. I looked across the drive at the compound, the unknown trees and big plants, the pile of rubbish that was lying next to the car that Uncle Jacques had collected us in.

'Where's Mum?' I asked.

'They've all gone into town. Miriam as well.'

I continued eating in silence. Aunt Céleste didn't say anything either, until I turned my gaze to her and was totally honest.

'*J'ai peur*,' I said, and when she smiled at me I frowned, and then she smiled more broadly. Small, white teeth. Big, brown lips.

'You must listen to your instincts,' she would later say, via the webcam. 'The things you feel are real, even though you can't give them a name.'

Listen to your instincts. Don't accept the rules of the world without questioning them. You're one of those children.

85

I began to cry. I was so sad. I had never been so sad. Shocked, Aunt Céleste pulled me onto her lap and I kept crying. She said something in French that I didn't understand and gave me a kiss on the cheek. That's what I'm thinking of now, that I said I was scared then.

The fear went away, of course. Because it had to. And I got used to things. Because I had to. It was *imperative*.

I played with Miriam and Antoine and Vivianne and Michel and Ruben and Dionne and I sat on the laps of all my uncles and aunts and I ate roasted peanuts, fish fried in banana leaf, fufu, the spicy sauces and the sweet fruit. I went along to the market, the sea, the city. I learned how to pester the goat and look out for snakes. In the end I didn't want to go home. That's how quickly it went.

Things tend to seem bigger than you first thought. After a while they no longer fit in the space they first occupied. Every time that confrontation with the fact that things aren't the way you'd understood them to be. That's the shock: that they no longer fit in the old spaces, that's the feeling of anxiety. The watch isn't in the drawer, the skin doesn't smell the same, the country isn't what you thought it was. You aren't even the person you thought you were. You can't hold on to it. You didn't get it right. You didn't see what you thought you were seeing.

WHEN WE WERE BACK in the Netherlands again I couldn't stop talking about Cameroon to Liliana and all the other children at school. I turned it into a paradise. I talked to everyone about it, compared it to the Netherlands, compared Africa to Europe. Everything was hotter, more beautiful, more colourful, sweeter, more, more, more. The picture's so lovely that you begin to believe it. That's why I understand Frits so well.

I'd created a beautiful image. Then the asylum seekers' centre came to the village and it all turned out to be completely different. When the centre arrived and the children had formed their own image of the world I'd told them about, mine was replaced by something else. Paradise didn't last.

One day I was walking through the village. This was when the asylum seekers' centre had just been set up. The teachers from our school tried to explain to us why people from the Middle East and Africa were coming to live here all of a sudden. What, asked Mr Bart the teacher, do you think you should do when you've fled your country because of war and you arrive in another country?

'Learn the language,' I said, 'then you can talk to the local people.' Then you can understand your aunt when she cracks a joke in Ewondo and you feel more at home with your uncle's 'r'.

Yes, the teacher said, but if you don't have a home what use is a new language then? Where are you going to do your homework?

'In the countries these children come from there's war,' said Mr Bart, 'war.'

I remember I felt ashamed at that point. There was no war in Cameroon. Or maybe there was. How should I know?

I only knew the big white house and the market. My uncle's house was in Cameroon and I had to talk French to make myself understood. It's where you woke up because you heard the birds screeching in the tree next to the house.

I'd gone to the village on my bike and bought sweets in Superdrug. I ate a sweet piece of liquorice while I scooped Smurfs, cherries and hearts into a plastic bag. I paid in coins and went outside. A man with long hair and gunge in his eyes came up to me, waved at me and said: '*Welcome* to the *Netherlands*!'

That's what I mean. Your train of thought gets distorted. You're being interrupted. Just when the images appear to follow on from each other in a logical sequence, that image is suddenly rejigged. You think there's peace and quiet, but then you look around you, and there's chaos instead. And you have to deal with that: the distortion, the fear, then the getting used to it, giving it space in your mind. Welcome to the Netherlands. Your children don't understand the culture. Or is she not able to speak?

IT'S A WEEK BEFORE MY FIRST temporary release day and Mum visits me on her own. Frits had said that we 'were making significant progress' and thinks I'll deserve a trip to the library soon, accompanied by a supervisor.

Mum looks tired. Carlita's daughter has been born, she tells me as soon as she comes in. She's called Faith and is gorgeous. Miriam's with her now, together with Alexandra, their other friend, and Miriam's new boyfriend, who lives in a swanky area at the edge of the village.

'He's a bit of a plonker, that Jeffrey,' says Mum when she pronounces the name of Miriam's boyfriend. 'I'd also give you your aunt's letter if I could, but as you know that's not possible.'

I'm not allowed to read the letters Aunt Céleste writes to me because they're in French and no one can check what's in them. I offered to translate them for Marco so that he could then check them for forbidden content.

'Don't be funny, you,' he said, waving me off.

'I'm serious,' I said. I left the office. 'I can translate what it says myself and then you guys can look at it?'

'And who says that you've earned such privileges?'

Splitting headache. Flashes in front of my eyes.

'But that's work, Marco,' I say slowly. 'Not a fucking privilege.'

'Ah,' I now say to Mum.

'In any case, at least Miriam's new boyfriend isn't one of those types from the writer's district.' The writer's district in our village is a working-class area where every so often a meth lab in someone's garage blows up. We live in an area where flats are interspersed with detached houses, where the streets are a little wider than over there. We live in a house, it's small but because Mum and Dad have bought it they think that's different.

89

'Are you looking forward to going to the library?' Mum asks.

'I think so,' I say.

'Maybe next time you can come home.'

'I hope so,' I say.

Mum smiles at me and I try and do the same.

'Why did we never go back to Cameroon?' I then ask.

Mum shrugs her shoulders, licks her lips.

'There was never enough money.'

'And now?'

'Now your father's ill.'

'Doesn't he want to go back, especially now? When he's better?'

'Things will have to improve first.'

'And then?'

'It depends on whether your father feels like it. He's never been in such a hurry.'

'Doesn't he miss our family then?'

'I think,' says Mum as if she has trouble with the words, 'that Dad finds family a bit difficult sometimes.'

'Oh,' I say, 'like Aunt Céleste?'

Mum remains silent for a long time.

'No, not Aunt Céleste. Not every woman's made for that kind of life,' she says. 'That of a housewife, I mean.'

'I get that.'

'I think she's much happier now.'

'And her children?'

Mum shrugs her shoulders again. In the past, when I asked Mum questions about plants or politics or why we never went on holiday, she'd tend to shrug her shoulders. She'd say: 'That's the way it is' or: 'I've no idea' and then I'd say: 'You're really stupid.' I've been thinking more and more recently that when Mum says that she doesn't know something, she's actually very good at seeing the difference between not knowing something and not wanting to know something, and that I, despite the fact that I always want to know everything, am in fact the stupid one.

'I want to see Aunt Céleste,' I say, 'when I'm out. In Barcelona.'

'We can't really go on a big holiday now, Salomé.'

'No,' I say, 'I want to go on my own.'

'On your own?' Mum looks surprised. 'Where did you get that idea from all of a sudden?'

'You know,' I say.

She looks at me as if she doesn't think it's such a bad idea.

'We can try and find out if Dad agrees and how much it'll cost,' she says. 'And we'll have to discuss it with the social worker.'

'Doesn't have to be immediately.'

'Why do you want to go anyway?'

'You know,' I say. 'I want to know what it's like.'

'What what's like?'

'That life. Aunt Céleste's.'

'Making a fresh start,' Mum says. Then we don't say anything for a moment.

She asks after the book by Jan Wolkers she's given me to read. I'd actually like to know more, ask more about Aunt Céleste, who made a fresh start, because I want to know how you do that. But Mum seems to think it's important we talk about books.

'Jan Wolkers,' I say, 'is nasty.'

It makes her laugh.

IN MY DREAM I'M NOT STUCK in the Donut, but I am locked up. In my dream I'm looking out of the window of a building and through that window I see a tall, black man standing at the barriers and he's looking over a field and everything glistens. In my dream he's wearing a long down coat and old trainers. He points upwards, from the field to the sky, the heavy, dark, overcast sky. In between two rain clouds a woman appears. She has enormous black wings and red eyes, scratched open. She's screeching. The sound echoes, comes from far. And then it gets louder, more shrill, more unbearable when she comes increasingly close. It makes the air tremble. I tremble.

'Look,' says the man in the down coat. When he turns his face towards me it's the same face as the woman's: bleeding eyes, brown, broken teeth, forked tongue, and that mouth, raw from all the screaming. The closer the woman gets to the earth the louder she screeches, furiously flapping her wings, and the man starts to join in. It thunders, their voices echo, they're so extremely fucking angry.

Jeering and then a loud crash. I hear a low voice shouting something. Someone knocks on my door. Thumps.

I sit up in bed.

'Who is it?' I call. I hear the peep of the automatic door lock and someone kicking it open with a bang, then running away. The embers of my dream are still flickering and I'm sweating. I look at my legs. I move them and they're working. Hands to my mouth and I don't have a mouth that's raw from screaming.

The light from the corridor hurts my eyes and just as I'm about to get up to close the door, Henny enters.

'What are you doing?' I ask angrily, squinting my eyes at her silhouette. 'What the fuck's going on?'

92

'They stole a pass.' Henny's stance suggests she's crushed.

'What?' I stare at her blue pyjama bottoms, her bare feet, the T-shirt hanging over her big breasts.

'They stole a pass from the supervisors,' she repeats. 'They came into my room and ripped off my blankets. One of them took my TV.'

It takes a moment for me to grasp that she's scared, Henny. I've no idea why she's come to me, but I lie down under the blankets again, pull up my legs and pat my hand on the mattress. She closes the door behind her and sits down.

'Are you okay?' I ask and turn on my bedside lamp. 'We'll just wait here until it's over.'

'Was quite a shock.' It's only now that I hear how high Henny's voice is. Her hands are small, her nails broken off. I hear a man's voice and more running, banging. An alarm goes off.

'If they come in here, I'll hit them with the lamp,' I say, pulling the lamp's plug out of its socket. Henny nods.

'Thanks.'

She looks at her hands. She's trembling. I work my way closer to her from underneath the blankets and put my arm around her shoulder.

'They've not done anything, right?' I ask.

'No, no,' replies Henny. 'Don't worry.' She suddenly looks very sad and it makes me all panicky.

The door swings open. Geert looks into my room, two big strides inside and grabs Henny roughly by the arm.

'What are you doing here?' he snarls. He's furious, you can tell instantly.

All of a sudden Henny looks really tiny, compared to that shit-face hanging over her.

'They came into her room,' I say when Henny doesn't respond. Geert hauls her up, off my mattress. Henny trips over my slippers and squeaks when she almost falls over but Geert ignores her.

'Go back to your room, you. And close your door,' he calls, pushing her into the corridor. I watch her run off, clumsily with those big, swaying breasts. Then he turns to me.

'And you, stay where you are.'

Someone runs past behind him and the man I don't know shouts 'Hey!' and Geert shouts 'God-*dammit!*' and then all three are gone. I go over to the window, gaze into the night.

It only lasts a moment. Three boys. Four? I hear Ashli shout. Marissa's loud laughter. Boys' voices swearing. Or maybe I don't notice them any more. We always hear them in fact, everywhere in the Donut. I lie down in bed again, the blankets over my head. I hear them screaming, as if in a frenzied trance. It reminds me of Friday night in the village. Crap crap crap, someone calls. More banging. Very quiet. I no longer sleep.

THE FOLLOWING MORNING, at breakfast, everyone's talking about it. How the boys from Unit B ran amok. How one of them stole the security pass, during a fight with a supervisor earlier in the week. How he waited till midnight, broke out of the isolation cell and with a few friends decided to riot. They sneaked through the Donut, ran into the corridors and found the way to our unit. They shook the bottles of pop as hard as they could, opened them and sprayed them all around, the fizz spurting against the ceiling; the alarm began to howl, the doors between the units closed automatically. They fought with the security guys near the exit and kicked a door down. One of the boys escaped and still hasn't been found.

'They were suddenly in my room,' Feline laughs. 'Really, what the fuck.' Geraldine's eating her muesli with trembling hands and Henny's not at breakfast. Marco isn't around, Ashli doesn't stop laughing. The director called in at the beginning of breakfast and cast furious glances around the table.

'If someone amongst you finds the pass, it's important you hand it over to one of us. We take this extremely seriously and so should you. We'll find out anyway if one of you has helped them.'

During lunch they search our rooms. One by one we have to stand in the doorway and look on while they pull books from the cupboard, yank posters off the wall, turn over mattresses and make-up bags. They find nothing. Then they're gone again.

Marissa can't stop talking about it when we do the laundry.

'So where were you?'

'In bed, what do you think?'

'Yo, I'd have killed to be with them,' she grins. She pushes her knickers into the big drum full of towels and clothes. 'Create a bit of mayhem in this shithole.'

'Why would you?' I ask more sharply than I meant to. 'You're almost out. Is that stupid or what?'

She frowns and shrugs her shoulders.

'Take it easy,' she says, and then: 'One of those guys has already given me what I wanted.' And I should leave it at that, but I shove my last T-shirts into the machine and slam the door shut.

'I don't need to hear that shit from you.'

'Take it fucking easy, yeah?' Marissa snaps, jumps up and positions herself right in front of me, her chest puffed up like an idiot. And all at once she's very tall, broad. She reminds me of the woman in my dream, the man.

'I *am* taking it fucking easy,' I say. I turn around, pick up the bottle of laundry detergent as calmly as possible and start to pour it into the washing-machine drawer. Marissa looks on, her hands clenched into fists. When I go to the recreation yard later, she isn't there. She already has what she wanted anyway.

NOW THAT THERE'S BEEN RIOTING by the boys, we're no longer allowed to meet up in the common room in the evening, only at the weekend. The pass has been found, I think; they have deactivated and replaced it. The boys aren't allowed to go out at all and no one can go on temporary release.

'We'll put your library visit off for a couple of weeks or so,' says Frits. 'For everyone's safety.'

'But I didn't do anything,' I say.

'It's not about you.'

Then he falls silent for a moment. I have, I realise, got used to talking to this man, in this office, the fences all around us. I'd set out to do something quite different.

'Compared to how you were when you came here, you've been remarkably calm lately,' says Frits.

'Yes,' I reply.

'Why's that?'

'What are you driving at?'

'I mean, is there a reason?'

'Isn't that the idea?' I ask. 'That I'm calm now?'

Frits scratches his chin, which reveals the beginnings of a grey goatee. The last few sessions we've talked about what I've done, how I ended up here. Every meeting sends me into a white rage. He pushes and pushes and I have to use all my energy to make sure I don't snap. I don't want to discuss it step by step. I can barely remember it.

'Yes,' he says, 'but even during all that disturbance over the past few days? I heard they kicked open the door to your room.'

'They didn't do anything.'

'Okay then,' he says. 'And that day? What went wrong there?'

97

We both don't say anything for a long time. Frits keeps staring at me.

'I was really angry.' I frown.

'No, but, I mean, I read the report.'

'What do you mean?'

'Where did you get the strength to do that?'

'We talked about that last time as well,' I say.

Last week Frits asked me to depict an image of what I call 'strength' and then I told him a bit about Dad. The café window, the car's wing mirror, how he threatens to hit Miriam when she gets at him. But what I reflected on later was his silence. The smoke coming from his nose with the fishing tackle on the table. My old aunt who said to him about me: she looks like you. Work hard. Don't moan.

'I'd like to pick up that conversation again,' says Frits.

I'm thinking about the front garden that I helped Dad tend, sneezing over the hydrangea because of hay fever. Mum's rose bush behind which Dad would listen to his cassettes on a portable stereo he'd placed on the ground, softly playing crackling old Congolese music, while he weeded. He smoked cigarettes sitting on a plastic stool from the garage. One summer, years ago, the man next door called me a shitty little black kid because there was always so much noise coming from our house. We laughed and talked too loudly or something. Miriam and I had a lot of fights on the drive, in the back garden. Too often, the doors were open. When I stare out of the window of Frits's office, I see Dad's glowing cigarette appear from behind the green and red, the clenched fists.

'With your fucking shouting and fucking music all day,' the next-door neighbour shouts at me. Straight at my face. I'm twelve. And I can see his hatred: in his wrinkles and the muscles in his jaws. His red face. Dad rises up from behind the flowers, calm as ever. Then he grabs the rake standing upright next to the stool and hisses that I should go. *Go.*

And I don't go, because I want to see it. I stay on the spot and watch how he crosses the garden: my dad. Samuel Atabong, six foot two, trampling on plants with his big workman's boots at the end of his bendy legs, cigarette between his lips and the rake in his raised hand. He runs towards the neighbour, whom he, as I hear later when he and Mum have a fight over it, threatens with death.

'What are you saying,' he thunders, 'to my daughter?'

The neighbour flees and Dad gives chase. He smashes his car windows, so it turns out, with the neighbour hiding in the house, looking on from behind the window. After that I never saw that man again, well, once: he turned around and cycled away at break-neck speed when he bumped into me. Mum was angry at first, but later it became a kind of family joke. Do you remember that time when?

Right *through* your enemy.

I miss this, that it's serious but also a joke, Dad's calmness when he draws a line. And then *thwack*. And then the fighting. And, when it happened at home, the making up. That above all.

'I'm quite strong,' I tell Frits. 'That's quite useful sometimes.'

'How do you mean useful?' he asks. He leans forward, elbows on the table.

'My father thought we should be able to defend ourselves.'

'Against whom?'

'People like you.' I say it before I realise.

Frits makes a strange move with his head, as if he has a disgusting taste in his mouth.

'I don't quite follow.'

This ain't exactly *The Cosby Show*, Miriam said.

'They used to think I was a boy when I was little,' I say. 'And that Miriam was an easy girl. Things happened. Things that weren't very nice.'

Frits opens and closes his mouth. He slowly picks up his pen and notes something down.

'That can't have been easy.'

'No,' I say. 'Can I ask you something?'

He nods.

'Why did you take part? In the show?'

He turns around in his office chair. It makes him appear a lot younger.

'I have to confess,' Frits says slowly, 'that I can't really remember. I'd been to Africa so many times and it seemed fun to take part in a show that was about my interests. I *love* Africa, you know.'

'Okay.'

'But it was all extremely banal. In the end it was all about entertainment. So not my thing. But the longer you spend in an environment like that, yes . . .' He sighs and I look at the map of Africa, with the drawing pins. 'Before you know, you're going along with it.'

I thought, said Miriam when I asked after the boy in the car, that he loved me.

Such a special girl, so exceptional, so clever.

Frits, who makes his way to farmer Bassa, in one of the first episodes of the show, and asks: 'Do you know the tribe called the *Herero* from *Namibia*?'

Bassa looks straight at the camera: 'Does this goon think we're in Namibia?'

'You remind me of my friends there,' says Frits cheerily, pointing towards a vague place in the distance. 'Such interesting people! Beautiful spot. Really. Beautiful!'

'Thank you,' says Bassa.

Frits nodding intensely. Thumbs up.

'I've had it with those men,' says Bassa to himself, going into his hut, 'they all think this is a theme park.'

This was obviously all translated afterwards.

'It all went so quickly,' Frits says. He sighs and crosses something out on his notepad. And I nod. And I say that I can understand it.

When, later on, I stride along the ever right-curving corridor, I notice that in fact I can't understand it at all. That I don't feel like understanding it. I feel like screaming and punching someone or something. Open mouth with broken, brown teeth. Blood from my eyes, steam from my nose. I explode. Where's the other Salomé? Where's she hanging out while I go to pieces here?

On the way to the recreation yard I meet Zainab. She's wearing pink bath slippers with white socks, a hole in her right-hand sock, at the big toe. She doesn't look at me, just stands still, in the middle of the corridor, which makes me stop in my tracks as well. A strange kind of stand-off, like in a Western.

'Shouldn't you be in class?' she asks.

'I need to smoke,' I say. I've trouble saying it. My throat is thick.

Zainab bites on her lip, her eyes hidden behind her black hair.

'I'll come with you,' she says.

We make our way over to the recreation yard in silence. No one's there. I offer her a cigarette and she takes it hesitantly from between my fingers, lets me hold the lighter at the end so that she only needs to inhale. She smokes quietly and I pace back and forth, from one wall to the other. My head fills with cancer. Cancer cancer cancer I want to shout. My whole life's stuffed with it. That shit's festering in my blood.

'I hate it here,' I say and give the cig bin a kick.

It topples dangerously and Zainab jumps aside. Then it slams back into place. A cloud of ash flies upwards.

'Sorry,' I say.

Zainab shrugs her shoulders. 'No, no need,' she says.

We smile at each other.

THAT WOMAN FROM MY DREAM, with those bloodshot eyes, those enormous black wings, that mouth. She descended towards the field, so screeching and fucking wild, like a Fury. She reminds me of Medusa, whose gaze turned you into stone, whose head was hacked off. Snakes for hair and those cold, piercing eyes, her mouth open as if she's constantly seeing things that make her gasp for breath.

Why was Medusa murdered in the first place? Had she deserved it? I can't remember. When I lie in bed, I see her face in front of me and I get it. I get it I totally get it. She at least is someone I understand.

Those Furies, the goddesses of retribution, were just as terrifying as the Gorgons according to Mrs Doormans who taught Classical Studies. They drove people who had committed terrible crimes to madness, for punishment, with their furious screeching, their repulsive appearance, the foul-smelling, putrid breath coming from their mouths. They came up from the underworld, half-woman, half-bird. Constantly back and forth between hell and here. What had the world done to them? What made them so furious? I want to know at what point the screeching began. Maybe they'd just been born angry, maybe the world they'd grown up in had given them every reason to be. Did they just want to be there, down below, but was it because of people that they couldn't stop themselves? We forced them the whole time to come up again.

The man with the down coat. Shitty little black kid. Monkey. It's not all about you. The way in which Miriam's friend grabbed her throat. With Aunt Céleste on the veranda in Cameroon. *J'ai peur. Très sec.* Henny on my bed in her blue pants. Frits with his friends in *Namibia*. All that crap here, in this place. It's not going away and will not be replaced by something else.

I think it started when we got back to the Netherlands, after the visit to our family in Cameroon, the feeling as if the weirdest images were linked, images that don't seem to have anything to do with each other.

You commit a murder and three Furies pursue you until you go mad. Three sisters, women, virgins, who're constantly waiting for someone to make a mistake. There's consistency in that. They're all causes with the same consequences.

I didn't understand the rules, when I got home again. I didn't shatter into pieces. I shrank. The fact that I didn't know the rules became a problem. The problem muzzled me. I didn't screech – far from it. It made me quiet. That's all it did.

The problem was the French CD-ROM course. The problem was *très sec*. It was the man who stood by the fence of the asylum seekers' centre in a down winter coat. A man boys threw coins at. It became as big as a village. It featured on TV. It said monkey. I mimic you. It screamed and had short white teeth, long crooked, yellow. It had a bloodthirsty, furious mouth. It had never pronounced my name correctly. It grew big and nasty and even shouted from a car at me. It even made Miriam look up with a start. Grabbed her neck. It was lying cut-price in a crate. The final edit was rather off. I ran away from it and tried to ignore it. I kept quiet when I could. When the man in the street with gunge in his eyes said: '*Welcome* to the *Netherlands*,' I said, as if it were the easiest thing in the world: 'Thank you very much.' Then I got up and said: 'Never.'

I no longer fitted the space I had originally occupied. It didn't pan out as I had understood it would. I hadn't seen what I thought I'd been seeing. The problem didn't go away. It tormented and battered. The problem was an attack, so I rose up, rod in hand. And the screeching. Ear-piercing screeching. I didn't moan, worked hard, and that wasn't enough.

IT'S QUIET OUTSIDE WHEN WE HIT the recreation yard on Saturday. Quieter than usual, when the boys play basketball or football and, right in front of the supervisors, games on phones that have been smuggled in. We've got the yard all to ourselves. For hours. No units playing football with each other. No rap numbers assaulting our ears through open windows. No trainers being kicked against big metal doors leading onto the yard. Marissa's playing basketball on her own. A few other girls are sitting on the ground. The sun's blazing, for the first time in weeks. There's a smell of flowers, even though they don't grow here.

On Sunday it's also sunny. Again it's quiet, inside as well. The furniture, the supervisors, the crows, the grass, the fence, everything's asleep. The boys, who encircle us from the other units in the Donut, are also asleep.

Marissa's asked Marco for permission and he's checked with the director and so she's allowed to be in my room with me. She has a bottle with pink cream, two big combs, two hairclips and a bunch of hairbands, and she throws everything onto my bed. Then she grabs the chair at my desk, places it in the middle of my room and points at it.

'Sit.'

Since our fight in the laundry room we've hardly talked to each other, but now she's standing in my room as if nothing's happened.

Marco's still hovering in the doorway. He points at the door.

'That's staying open,' he says. I nod and Marissa nods and then he's gone and she rolls her eyes.

'Sit,' she says again. She looks around my room.

It's only now that I get how bare it is, because Marissa looks so surprised. The only thing you can say about my room is that there are books. Mum keeps bringing them and I keep reading them. The walls are still white, without posters or cards. There's nothing on the shelves of the open cupboard next to my desk other than clothes, and there isn't even anything on the desk apart from the ten new and old and big and small books that are allowed.

'Don't you have a stereo or something?' Marissa asks, as she goes over to the window and opens it. She's holding the big, black Afro comb like a weapon and I see her eyes wandering from the view to the titles.

'No,' I say.

'How do you listen to music then?' She picks up part four of Harry Potter, the part in which Voldemort returns to the grave-yard and Cedric Diggory dies, and then after having turned it over, puts it back.

'Well, I guess I don't,' I say.

'Shit.'

'Sorry.'

'No, no,' she says, laughing airily. 'It's okay. I just thought, then we'll do your hair and listen to some music.'

'I hadn't given it any thought.'

'It's cool. I'll get mine.' She throws the comb onto the bed and leaves the room. I remain standing in my room, which only now seems to take actual shape, a shape that embarrasses me. When Marissa returns she's carrying a small stereo and some CDs.

'My brother's,' she says, shoving a few books aside with her arm and putting the stereo on the desk. She sticks the plug in the socket, presses play and turns up the volume. Chingy.

'Your hair,' she says, 'is real faktap.'

The pink stuff she puts in my hair smells sweet, of coconut and something flowery. She pulls my hair apart with long strokes, slaps a dollop of cream in the palm of her hand and rubs it into my curls. She's careful, and when she pulls too hard and my head jerks backwards, I swear and she laughs.

'You really should look after yourself better, dude.'

'I know.'

'When did you last go to the hairdressers?'

I don't want to tell her that Dad cuts my hair, so I shrug my shoulders.

Marissa combs out my hair for two hours, separating it with hairclips, from the bottom of my neck to the hairs on my forehead. She raps along with Lloyd Banks and Snoop Dogg and Kanye West, continually changing CDs on the stereo. We sing along together in funny voices to the numbers we both know. At times I almost drop off, when my hair's been untangled and the combing almost feels like a massage.

When Marissa's nearly done she stands in front of me and I look at her Nike jumper and the golden crucifix around her neck, the tattoos on the inside of her muscular arms. When all the tangles have been removed, she divides my hair into two sections and plaits right down to my neck, puts hairbands around the end of the plaits.

'Your hair's kind of long, man,' she says, lifting my braids and draping them over my shoulders. She rests her hands there for a moment. I move my fingertips to the hairbands resting against my collarbone and admire the bits of shining hair I can see.

'Yes,' I say, 'funny to see it like this, in fact.'

Marissa squeezes my shoulders and begins to put away her things.

'Time for a smoke.'

I go over to the mirror and look. My face's naked like this, with my hair out of the way. My two scars contrast sharply with my pale skin. I yawn at length and expansively, with my arms above my head, like at home when, on Sundays, I've binge-watched MTV marathons of *Pimp My Ride* or *The Hills* for hours and finally get up to fetch some crisps, and then I say, yes, let's do that. Without pressing the stop button Marissa pulls the plug from the socket, cutting Common off mid-verse. We trudge to the recreation yard, which is empty and hit by a last few rays of sunshine. Marissa throws her lighter into the air, against the steel of the fence above our head, and the pigeon that was there flies away after dropping a wet blob on the ground that makes us flinch.

'Thanks for my hair,' I say, rubbing my hands over the burning baby hairs. They've been pulled tightly into the plait and are damp from the hair stuff.

'No worries,' she says. I offer her a cigarette and we smoke. Marissa blows out smoke rings. We aren't really saying anything. During our second cigarette I briefly put my head on her shoulder, which she allows. When we've finished we go indoors for a Coke. The rest of the Sunday drags past like treacle. In the common room it's quiet aside from the TV, and in the corridors there's no music or shouting. No boys. It's almost scary. With my face in the sun on the sofa it almost feels like home. I don't want that, but there's nothing I can do about it.

THE FOLLOWING DAY THE SUN'S out in full force. The warm air pushes itself into the Donut and leaves the classrooms, my room, the common room with a stale aura. As if the oxygen has been sucked out of it. There are girls everywhere: hanging around the walls of the recreation yard, gossiping underneath the basketball net. Zainab's sitting on her own against the wall of our recreation yard.

Marissa dribbles the basketball back and forth, shaking her head. I don't take this game seriously. She aims the ball at my head but misses.

'Stupid bitch.'

'Fuckwit.' I grin and Marissa grins back.

'Stop pissing about, yeah,' she says. The ball's landed near Zainab, she picks it up and bounces it in my direction.

'Want to join in?' I ask.

'No thanks.' She's wearing ear studs and tilts her face towards the sun. I dribble back to Marissa and go and stand next to her, aim for the net and miss.

'Have you seen *Total Recall*?' she asks, picking up the ball. She aims for the net and the ball eases through it. I pick it up, shoot, and miss again. The ball bounces towards the waste bin where Feline, Ashli and Geraldine are. When I slip past them Ashli spits on the ground but I don't respond.

'Have you see *Ten Things I Hate About You*?' I call over my shoulder instead. There's some mumbling. I clasp the ball between my arm and my side.

'What kind of dumb title is that?' Marissa calls back.

'It's a romcom,' I say.

'What the fuck's a romcom?' Marissa grins and stops in the middle of the yard with her hands in her pockets. I love that grin.

That grin feels like jumping off a high board into a sheet of flames. I will miss her when she's gone.

'A romantic comedy, idiot,' I say.

'Why should I watch that shit?'

I shrug my shoulders and throw the ball back at her. She catches it easily.

'Have you seen *Brick*?' I ask.

'Get out of my way,' Ashli says.

'Is that also a romcom?' Marissa asks.

'No, you'd love it. It's about a boy in the States and his girlfriend goes missing and—' Ashli pushes my shoulder and I go with the motion but I keep my balance.

'Don't touch me,' I say.

'Go and talk to your boyfriend over there,' she says. The group laughs.

'So it's a fucking romcom,' says Marissa. She heaves an exaggerated sigh.

'No one said it was a comedy, dickhead. It's about drug dealers. That film's nice.'

'So it's all about love then.'

'How do you know?'

'She goes missing? His girlfriend? Ain't that the reason for everything? If that's the beginning, and the reason, then it's a romantic film, right?'

There's some sniggering when I don't reply. I roll my eyes. Since Marissa did my hair on Sunday some girls have been cracking jokes. I don't mind, and I'm used to people taking the piss out of me. They're afraid of Marissa because Marissa does press-ups in her room before she goes to sleep. I don't think they're afraid of me, but I never say anything and they think that's weird. Weird can be good too sometimes.

'The fact that the hero of the story takes action because someone he loves is in trouble doesn't mean it's a love story. Then every action film would be a love story. Then Bruce Willis would be the Hugh Grant of America,' I shout, passing her the ball.

'Who the fuck's Hugh Grant?' asks Marissa. She laughs

uncomfortably and returns the ball, but she aims at Ashli. I catch it just before it hits Ashli in the face.

'Fuck off,' she says.

'Fuck you,' I say. I shoot the ball to the net and it bounces off the edge. Marissa laughs at me and the group laughs at me, but that sound, missing the net, the bounce against the metal ring, makes me feel tired again. I take a step forward and it's as if I'm wading through water. I move away from the group and they spit at me. Marissa begins to roar with laughter as she runs after the ball and, instead of picking it up, kicks it against the fence. The shoe on the foot she kicks with flies off in the process. Savanna feebly whimpers something about order. Marissa hops to the shoe and, once she's shoved her foot into it, goes over to the ball. It's weather for playing basketball, not for fighting with Ashli or thinking about Dad. That's what I was thinking about this morning, when I woke up.

In the summer I feel like sitting in front of a fan and listening to music, eating watermelon, drinking tea with honey, hearing the children in the neighbourhood play.

'When I get out of here for the first week I'll just drink energy drinks and eat chips,' says Marissa when we have walked over to each other. I sit down on the tarmac. I don't know what I'll do when I'm no longer here. Whether I'll feel like eating. Marissa talking about leaving tires me out.

'Have you seen *The Fast and the Furious*?' she asks. I start to laugh. I've seen *The Fast and the Furious* loads of times. She laughs with me, but apprehensively.

With Liliana, whom I've known since primary school, I'd eat bags of Cheetos and drink iced tea while watching Paul Walker race around in expensive cars. When her parents were at home, her father was usually having a nap on the sofa and her mother would be smoking cigarettes in the kitchen listening to a Polish radio station on the PC.

Dad's never liked Liliana, even though she's my only friend. This is because her parents allow her to stay out late and she's often hanging around with her brothers and cousins in the playground next to the small mosque in our area. It's also because her eldest brother's one of the dudes who tends to be arrested when another meth lab blows up in the village. It's also because she's never phoned me once since I was arrested. Not that Dad's come to see me either as yet.

'Have you seen 2 *Fast* 2 *Furious* then?' I ask

'Sure,' says Marissa, 'with Tyrese.'

'He was hot,' I say.

'I liked Vin Diesel more. Ludacris was also hot.'

'Yes,' I say, but now I'm really knackered. Marissa launches into some breakdancing. I watch it, sitting cross-legged. She comes towards me balancing on her hands and moving her legs in the air. Her plaits flap against her back, cheeks and shoulders. She moves nimbly. Marissa's broad, muscular. Straight. She somersaults and lands cleanly, sinks a little through her knees when she realises she isn't going to fall.

'I fancy a joint,' she says.

'Okay.'

'Sorry.'

'I just want to sleep, man,' I say.

'Grinch.' Marissa begins to whistle.

Geert taps his watch.

'Time to go,' he shouts at us. The boys are allowed out in the yard in a minute. For the first time since the riot.

'I've got class,' I say, getting up.

'Yeah, you go back to school, yeah,' Marissa says.

I wipe my trousers and go in, alone, instead of lingering and stretching time outside as long as possible as I usually do. It's spring now. Pollen's flying through the air.

Ashli, who's following me inside, shoves me in the back.

'Get a move on, lesbo.'

I hear Feline laugh. She cackles like a stupid bird. I kick backwards but don't touch anything.

'Bitch,' I mumble, but I can't get myself to sound angry.

'So what are you going to do?' Ashli laughs, walking past me. I imagine grabbing her by the hair and dragging her into the yard, bashing her head until there's no more face.

I look over my shoulder and see Marissa do another handstand. Her plaits drag along the ground as she starts walking on her hands towards the fence. I wonder if Ashli's holding back because Marissa's around.

Inside it's warmer than out, but there's no sun. In the corridor, on the way to the classroom, it's quiet.

THERE ARE THINGS IN MY HEAD that have started to connect. The holiday in Cameroon, the man at the gate. And that all I wanted to do was read. How I learned to hit a punchball and that I began to feel embarrassed about everything, my face, my hair, my name. It's so boring, so lame, so sad and so small when I think about it. It's not big at all. It's not mind-blowing.

'There's this track by Radiohead,' I say, and Frits looks up as if coming out of a deep sleep. 'Do you know Radiohead?'

'Yes,' says Frits, 'as in "Creep".'

'Brilliant band,' I say and look at my nails, wide and bitten to the quick, and then at the floor.

'Which track?' says Frits. He's wearing a jumper today. It's blue with a brand name on it. And I don't know, but it does something to me, that jumper this man put on. I just want to go home. It's a sensation I've been feeling very strongly all day.

'All my pasts and futures,' I say.

'Is that what the song is called?'

'No. There's this track, "Pyramid Song", sung by Thom Yorke. "There was nothing to fear and nothing to doubt", and it's so beautiful.'

'I don't think I know it,' says Frits.

'"Pyramid Song",' I say. I feel the urge to cry. I want to go home and put on a jumper because it's cold. Open my wardrobe and find that everything in it is mine.

'Why do you like that track?'

'Because it's sung in the past tense. As if all good things have been accomplished and he's happy with that and wants to tell people about it.'

'Because it's behind him?'

'Yes. Because it's good. You know.'

'Tell me why,' he says.

'No,' I say.

I have to think of Miriam and how she spat in my face, and of Mum, who could only shake her head, with her mouth wide open, and Dad at the dining table with his hands covering his eyes, a burning cigarette between index and middle finger. When we phoned yesterday he said: 'Things are going well' and I didn't believe him.

'Why not?'

'Sorry?' I say.

'Why don't you want to tell me why?' Frits asks. 'Do you feel guilty?'

'Never,' I say.

In the courtroom when I had to keep my mouth shut and let the lawyer do the work I said the same. The prosecutor mispronounced my name when he was presenting his case and I had to keep my mouth shut, but I said: 'Never,' I said I'd never feel sorry, not my whole fucking life.

'Because they don't feel guilty, so why should I?'

'You mean the boys?'

'Yes.'

'How do you know they don't feel guilty?'

'Well,' I say and take a deep breath, 'I just know for sure.'

'Because they've not been punished?'

'They have,' I say.

Frits opens his mouth, closes it again, frowns.

'I punished them,' I say, and tap my index finger just above my breast, and Frits shakes his head, notes something down. If there was any logic in it, this would surely be it? That I've punished them? Because if that's the case, then it should've turned out like in a Greek tragedy, and all those writers who wrote their books in the past tense – that's the way it happened and that's why it went like that – then isn't that the basis of the idea I'll understand in the end, that even if it's too late, it should end with punishment? That's how it ended with me, right?

Or like with the man in *The Stranger* who refuses to admit

there's a reason why he murdered the Arab? It was the sun. It was the wine. It was the day. The phases of the moon. It was my breakfast. Blah blah blah. It was nothing actually. I just did it. I saw a chance and I did it. Was that the way it happened?

Frits says: if all those things are going around inside you and you can't find a way to let go, you'll come a cropper at some point.

That man, from *The Stranger*, Meursault, got one thing wrong. He needn't have killed the Arab. That didn't help one bit. Afterwards the sun only burnt more fiercely and the man hadn't deserved it. He didn't have a good reason. He just felt like it. But that wasn't the most important thing. What was most important was that it didn't change anything. Nothing changed at all. And even though I don't feel sorry, that's why I go crazy here. Even though you rise up out of your pit every so often, screaming, rod in hand. Even though you break with the story and you do things your own way. Even though you surrender. Even though you work your guts out. Even though you had the feeling that you needed it. Even though you never moaned, never ever. In the end you are exhausted and you descend again. Someone gets punished and everything else just carries on. No one learns anything. A blanket draped over the pit muffles the screaming.

Why did he do it? What difference does it make anyway? He should've stayed calm and lain down in the sand. I should've stayed calm and remained in the water. Let my schoolbooks get soaked in the ditch. Or perhaps that idea's too naïve.

'Is that the way you see it, that you've punished them?' Frits asks slowly, lifting his head from his writing.

'What I like so much about that track,' I say, 'is that it's all past history. But more than that really, that there's harmony. That there's harmony and that it's good. That it's right.'

That it led somewhere. That the endpoint has been reached and that things are right there. That, at some point, you'll hear that it served a useful purpose, what you did. That it led somewhere, even though you've been punished. That's what I want to tell him.

'But you understand that it's not up to you, don't you?' Frits says.

'Up to whom then?' I say. 'If they do something to me, I can give it back to them, can't I?'

'Eye for an eye.'

'No,' I said, 'over and done with. It had to stop.'

He clicks his biro in and out and writes. I slouch further.

'I really think that,' I say.

'And did it stop?'

I gaze out of the window. The puddles and the grass that sucks up water and drinks itself green. This fucking man.

'I've never interfered with anyone. And they don't interfere with me. They insult me. They steal from me. They ridicule me. And then I should leave it to someone else to do something about that?'

'What I'm getting at,' says Frits, 'is that you didn't need to solve it like that. Because I know you're better than that.' He looks outside, to the rain that's starting to fall, increasingly intensely, and then thrum against the windows.

'How do you know?' I ask.

'I just know,' he says, looking a little sad. And I wonder why I hadn't just carried on pounding then and jumped in front of a car. Disappeared. Or simply had let it happen, waited in the water until they went away, till evening fell, and sunk ever deeper into the ditch in the night, maybe even drowned. I'd have done everyone a favour. My family. It doesn't change anything anyway. We've already disintegrated. Miriam's the only one who has a lust for life. She's going to university, moving away from here. She'll probably manage. The things you leave behind are like wet cement, you pull yourself out of it before it sets, that's the opposite of what I've done. Miriam will have liberated herself soon, from the village, from me. And then you're someone who went away. Then you're lighter than the rest, you're able to fly.

I, on the other hand, am stuck in a pit. Mum and Dad are stuck in a pit. I'm just sick of it, that all the things that've happened to us seem false, strange, something to feel embarrassed about.

'I'm no better than anybody or anything else,' I say. Frits sits quietly at his desk. He looks like he's made of stone. Fat, pale fingers. The folds of the bags under his eyes. He sits still and breathes slowly.

'Okay then,' he says.

These days, when I look at Frits, I no longer see what I saw first. I no longer see a freak with long hair or a shitface from the TV. I just see a stupid old man. A nonentity.

AUNT CÉLESTE DIVORCED UNCLE HONORÉ. Miriam went to secondary school. I did the grammar school entrance exam and went to St Odulf's, in the small city ten kilometres away from the village. Miriam thought I talked posh, with my fancy fucking words I'd learned at grammar school. I don't want to talk, I said, I just want to be left in peace. Dad was sacked and there were arguments about money. Nothing about this is impressive. And yet it didn't fit the mould it occupied before. I tried to figure out: at which point would I have been able to take action, so that it didn't lead to this point?

There's no harmony. I can't come up with anything, like with Miriam and the boys in the car, like with Frits, so that I can understand it, even vaguely, somewhere far off. Which would make it fit.

When I sit on the bed looking at the wall opposite, when I'm not reading or thinking or anything, I turn on the tape and press play. Then the events follow in sequence the way they happened. Then it's not a structure. It isn't self-evident. There's no confrontation between how it was and how it is.

So I stare at the white wall. When I stare, I usually sit the way I sit now, or I lie stretched out on my side, my head leaning on my left underarm. I want to see as little as possible apart from the white, the least possible distraction. Sometimes I sit cross-legged facing the wall and don't think. It's the only thing that helps. I think that maybe, when I really work at it, I can let everything go, like the Buddhist monks we saw in a documentary last year during RE. Those monks who can go without food or water, who can withstand terrible pain, just by meditating. The focus on nothing. Silence. No language or sound or feeling or darkness, light, thundery rain, no money or love even. A big, white nothing which I'm so much part of that I'm nothing and then, in the end, that I don't even feel anything any longer. That's what I want. Then the images are no longer about me. I'm not aware, not of the birds singing, not of the air filter buzzing in my room, or the urge to drink or pee. I've disappeared into my own head. The blanket's covering the pit.

But my head does its own thing and returns to those places: Aunt Céleste's lap, the man with gunge in his eyes, that afternoon on the way home and how the boys overtook me. These are my things. These are things that I know. And I take them with me. I'll never get rid of them.

But the idea's that, with an awful lot of concentration, there's this point I can get to without all that shit, without all those people, without the things – I no longer know what they mean, the things I saw. I visualise this point as a meadow, bordering a forest, far away. I've not found the way to that place yet. I will get there. I have an idea what it'll look like when I find it.

But I mustn't think of my knuckles. I mustn't think of my teeth. Of those glistening coins at that man's feet. I mustn't think of the day it began. When everything began to talk to me. When the memories began to haunt me. They talk to each other. I can't get a word in edgeways. There's nothing I can do about it. When more turn up I push them away. Away with those monkey sounds. Away with the laughter. Away with the gnawing noise in the spot where they huddle together, mean and content, where they grow bigger until they bang against the walls of the pit. I push them away with music and by counting paving stones and focussing on a particular page in a book. Then they start whispering to me. I don't want to listen, but their voices get louder. If I don't pay attention the thoughts form a group. The group is inside me but I don't understand the rules.

I want harmony. I want to look away from the water. I don't want the boulder. I want to be left alone and go boating and stargaze and for things to be easy. I want it to be okay to do that. I want to go home. I wish I hadn't done anything. That I wasn't thinking I could stop it. That I was calm, a monk. That I was another Salomé, light, that I'm not bothered by anything at all. Out of the pit. Wash myself. Not have a fright when I see myself in the mirror. Walk out of my frame. No screeching around me. Just silence. End of the film.

'LOOK,' SAYS THE MAN, and the woman, the Fury, descends and screeches my name: Salomé Salomé Salomé! and he screeches in unison. I look on. And the down coat turns out to be a pelt. The man changes into a beast like her, with those black wings, his eyes start to bleed, their stench I can smell all the way over here. Together they approach me and the field they fly over scorches under the flapping of their wings. Everything behind them is withered, dead, burns down in one huge fire: the birds fall down sparks firing, the trees explode into clouds of ash. They're furious with me. They want to drive me crazy. They want me dead, dead like the falling birds, dead like the screaming insects, the panicking animals who burn to death in the forest. The screeching cracks the glass of the space I'm in. Two legs that don't want to move. The shards fly around me and I want to run away, but I can't do anything, I stagger, I fall. The man and the Fury come towards me, slobbering. Just as their claws clasp my legs, I fall into the abyss, as if the ground's opening up in front of me, as if the underworld wants my flesh. I want to keep on falling, but it's not enough. The man and the woman, the animals, they fall with me, screeching, but they're faster, heavier than me. They overtake me. When the darkness is everywhere, the fire so far above our heads, they've got me. The woman digs her claws into my skull and the man into my shoulders, they begin to pull, pull. They pull so hard. I feel it in the skin of my neck, my flesh, my muscles. They pull my head off.

I'M ON THE PHONE TO MIRIAM. For ten minutes. She says that Mum's cooking and that Dad's in the garage fiddling with his fishing tackle. That he's going fishing this weekend, with Peter, his best friend.

'How are you?' I ask.

'Good,' she says. 'I've got to scoop poo every morning, because all the neighbours let their dogs shit on the drive now that you're locked up. Not to make you feel bad, but that's the way it is.'

'Thanks.'

'Mum says I shouldn't really tell you, but I thought you should know.'

I close my eyes for a second and clench my jaws. 'Sorry I made your life difficult.'

'Thanks for the apology.'

I count to ten and say: 'Fuck you.' Then I ask after Dad. Miriam says that he's lost weight and is tired. That she heard him cry in bed the other night while Mum and him were whispering to each other. She asks if I want to speak to him and I say yes. I hear her walk over to the garage. I have a headache. I'm not having a good day today.

There's music from the radio Dad has in the garage. Then he comes on the phone. I suddenly feel very hot and get a lump in my throat as if I'll have to cry at any moment.

'How are you?' he asks.

'Fine,' I say. 'And you?'

'I dreamt about you,' he says.

'How?'

'I dreamt that you got onto a boat which was sailing away just as I got to the port to wave you off. And that Mum fell into the water when you called.'

'Oh,' I say.

'Very strange,' he says. Then: 'Things are going well. We're going fishing tomorrow. I've prepared everything.'

He starts to talk about his fishing rods and what the tide'll be like, because they're going out to sea, he and Peter, Peter of the samurai swords on the wall, to a place near where Grandma and Granddad used to live, near Vlissingen. It doesn't interest me all that much but I'm so glad to hear him. It also makes me so sad I have trouble swallowing.

'How's school?' he then asks. I only have a few minutes left.

'I had to write a poem,' I say, 'so I wrote about the back garden in summer.' That isn't true. Marissa wrote that poem. I was sulking and threw balls of paper at Ashli and Feline and called the teacher a fucking tart because Marissa's poem almost made me cry.

'That sounds nice,' says Dad. 'Great that you do those kinds of things in there.'

When we ring off I go over to my room as quickly as possible and throw myself onto the bed, scream into my pillow. Then I go to the recreation yard and smoke cigarette after cigarette.

WE'RE WATCHING *TWO WEEKS NOTICE* together. Honestly, I don't think the film's that bad. But Marissa's being a real pain. I've done it myself. It's not the first time I've seen it either. Once in a while, one by one, we go crazy. We riot and rant and rave. Sometimes because we're having our periods, sometimes because of lousy sessions with Frits. When girls know that they're close to being let out, it can also drive them crazy, they get cocky and go wild. Marissa's almost out. That's what I mean. Instead of watching, she rocks back and forth on her chair.

'What a pile of shit, that film,' she shouted, entering the common room. Marco said that she shouldn't stomp around so much. Now she's throwing cheese and onion crisps at the screen. One by one. Really. Geert gets up, grabs the bag from the table and puts it near Henny and Geraldine.

'Pile of shit,' Marissa repeats, very loudly. She gets up and goes over to the fridge.

I've brought a book, but the film's too good. Nobody dies and the people don't have such terrible problems. That calms me down. That's what I need.

Marissa has a glass of Coke and slurps it, throws kissing noises at the film when Sandra Bullock and Hugh Grant have a chat in a walk-in wardrobe.

'Marissa, can you be quiet for a moment?' says Geert. She goes '*tsk!*' clicks her tongue very loudly. Then she looks at me and pulls a funny face. I don't respond. I just want to watch Sandra Bullock. Marissa rocks back and forth on that crappy chair, with her arm leaning on the side table next to her, and Geert warns her one more time.

'I'll just sit how I want, yeah?' she says. 'What are you going to do?'

Geert gets up.

'Sit. Normally,' he says. Someone grabs the remote and turns up the volume of the film.

'You can't tell me what to do,' Marissa shouts. 'When I'm gone from here I do everything I want! Fuck you and your—' Blah blah blah. She goes on and on. It looks so dumb really. That's what strikes me now. When we have a go at the supervisors or at each other, when we kick the cig bin or slam the phone down on the table after we've spoken to our parents, we actually all look so fucking dumb.

'Marissa, I want you to sit down properly and not ruin the atmosphere for everyone else,' says Geert. Marco gets up and pushes the back of the chair down to make her sit straight, but the legs fly away from underneath her because of the slippery lino and she smashes backwards. Hard. I hear the thump of her head, or perhaps it was the timber of the chair, against the ground.

'Shite,' she screams, and it's quiet for a moment. Sandra Bullock says that Hugh Grant is 'the most selfish human on the planet'. I get up. Henny rubs her hands together and Ashli bursts out laughing. Marco reaches over to Marissa to help her up, but I feel it before I see it. Marissa's angry. She grips his arm and hits him with the flat of her hand in the face.

'Fucking wanker!'

Marco swears back.

'Easy,' Geert calls.

'Watch out,' I hear myself say, 'watch out watch out.'

Marco grabs her by the collar and lifts her off the overturned chair. Marissa wrestles herself free from him and wants to fight. Marco too, and Marco's got Geert next to him. Feline walks away, simply away, and Ashli cackles like some kind of deranged bird of prey.

'Easy!' Geert calls again, and they hold her back, both jumping onto her. The table gets knocked over and her ankle stays hooked behind a diagonal table leg as she fights off Marco and Geert. Once again Marissa falls backwards.

'Watch her head, man!' I shout.

'Shut it, you!' Marco screams. Geert reaches for the table, but Marissa's too strong. I develop a sudden headache, a *splitting* headache. Without realising I've moved closer and closer to the fight. I see myself lying there. Instead of Marissa and the supervisors, it's me with those boys hanging over me when they butt me in the stomach and face, me soaking from the water in the ditch, my chin already cut open, my bowels feeling like a big snake-like knot that's being butted and butted and butted, and just when Marissa gathers so much strength that she worms herself out of Marco and Geert's grip, that's the moment when I want it to stop, when I grab Paul by the throat with my one hand, while I clench the other one into a fist.

'Fucking wanker,' I coughed, and blood splattered in his face.

'Fucking wankers,' Marissa shouts again, and she starts hitting, long, flailing punches at Marco's face. It all happens so quickly. Screaming, crying, flat against the floor and all that shit. I crawl over to the first weapon I can find and it's a stick. Marco's arm around her neck. Geert kneeling on top of her. Something cracks, someone screams, but where? You blink and it's gone. The clunky racket, the thuds, the grating noises from the furniture people are falling against. They overpower her by throwing her onto her stomach and sitting down on her back. I'll kill you, I screamed. A fist on leather. I was used to that. It felt very different. Are you going to calm down, now? they keep asking. Are you going to calm down now? I will fucking kill you.

Marissa starts to cry, she nods.

'Is she okay?' I ask through my tears.

'Stay out of it,' Marco snarls, and he slowly gets off her back, takes her with him. Geert picks up the remote, turns off the TV and gestures to us to get up.

'To your rooms, all of you.' I turn around. Zainab's still staring at the screen. Ashli studies the tips of her hair with a face that's far too calm, and Henny has her hand over her mouth. The rest, the bitches I care about even less, look at me or at their shoes and I wipe away my tears with my lower arms.

'I said to your rooms!' Geert shouts.

'But it's film night,' someone sighs wearily.

Zainab rises from her chair by the window and goes over to the cabinet with the TV in it. She presses a button on the DVD player, removes the DVD and puts it in its case.

'Get a move on, now!' Geert screams. Henny's the first to go, then the rest trudge on behind her. My gaze follows Zainab, who, as quiet as a fox, slinks over to the fridge. She opens the door, gets a bottle of orangeade, pours herself a glass she's picked up from the drying rack and drinks in it one gulp, with her back leaning against the counter top, the fridge door still open. Geert straightens Marissa's chair and throws me an angry glare.

Only when I leave the room, tagging after the others into the corridor, does Zainab put her glass down and follow.

When I'm in my room I slam the door shut, grab my tube of hand cream and fling it against the wall, but it doesn't do anything. Then I grab *Harry Potter* and *Beloved* and that shitty Willem Frederik Hermans novel, the covers thumping against the wall. My bottle of deodorant and the alarm clock and the lamp on my bedside table, I hurl them one by one, as hard as I can against the white wall. Dull thud. Piercing bang. Shards. The sound of breaking plastic. The alarm clock bounces off the wall, hits my shin hard. I scream open-mouthed. I scream that I hate them all, the whole fucking lot of them. I stamp on it. I want everything to break apart until the end of times. For everything to disappear. For everything to be swamped. For it to blow away. For all gods in the world to be inflamed with wrath. For it to motherfucking burn.

I DON'T REGRET IT, that's it. I'm not sorry. That I'm not sorry and that no one thinks it's strange that I'm here is a blanket that's being draped over the edges of the pit. It makes it dark and the darkness makes me still. I'm so still that I no longer know how deep down I'm stuck.

You can only have ten books and ten magazines in your room. This means that, once it's been checked by a supervisor, I return each book that I've finished reading to Mum during visiting time. And Mum has another book inspected and that ends up on my bedside table again. I can never leaf back through something. Time doesn't give a fuck about all the things I want to reflect on a bit longer. In one of the books I read the main character says that each time you make an important decision, you leave a part of yourself behind, a part that continues to lead your old life as you get entangled in the consequences of the choice you just made. But I don't know if I can see it like that. Because I'm here. That's why everything revolves around the past. The future's broken. I see nothing when I look ahead, that's why I only look backwards. I'm stuck deep down in darkness. Time moves on but nothing happens. No, I don't believe what she says in the book.

The other Salomé who drinks tea with Queen Elizabeth, sets up a punk band in Paris. She doesn't do memories. She dwells in the light. When you leaf back, with all the knowledge of hindsight, it does not say what you thought it did.

THE DAY, TWO YEARS AGO in October, that Dad was sacked from the furniture factory following an argument with his boss that got out of hand, about a promotion he was due to get but which went to someone else, that's when it started, the fighting.

The clock, which began to tick in another tempo without telling us, that was fighting. I can still see Dad sitting in his chair, dazed. Bailiffs ringing the bell, with papers in a blue folder, looking past me into the hallway, that's fighting.

Not being allowed to take calls from unknown numbers, Mum crying in the car on the way to the supermarket on Saturday, Miriam disappearing time after time to Carlita or Alexandra, to boys from surrounding villages or in town.

You mustn't think you're alone.

It's not all about how *you* feel.

I can't explain the exact order of things, only that it was necessary to cycle through the fields alone instead of going to school and that it felt like a fist on a punchball, a fist against a cheek.

Me eating my lunch on the loo, my ears plugged against all the discordant screaming. I didn't have any real friends, and the friends I had forgot about me because I was never there.

The clock started to tick differently and every second beat was black: my mother's best friend died of a heart attack, that was in Year 7. I worked hard.

The fights started and lasted for days, then the silences you had to run away from. Miriam stealing money from Mum's bag, me threatening her with a knife when I caught her in the act.

Why are you doing all that? Why are you only making things worse?

You mustn't think you're alone. Even though you're trying to disappear. Don't moan. Work hard.

I cycled to town and traipsed through the shopping streets, slipped into shops for warmth and pocketed all kinds of nonsense, just to kill time.

Because I was always playing truant, I stood out when I was in school. I tried to evaporate. I no longer studied and I had to keep retaking my year, but that didn't solve anything.

My face was glued onto the bodies of naked women in dirty magazines, plastered onto locker doors. That was Year 8. I didn't moan. My backpack emptied into the bin, my clothes put in the shower during PE. Then the tap was turned on. I didn't moan.

You only need two people with bad intentions. You only need two people and an outsider as a target and the rest follows of its own accord.

When I tell Frits this, he says: 'That must've been very difficult for you.'

I've kicked so many bikes to bits. I've plucked so many mobiles from the front pockets of bags. I chucked them all into the canal. I've plugged my ears, but the screeching's discordant and doesn't stop.

Paul and Salvatore, the farmer and the Italian from my class, called the landline to tell my stay-at-home Dad or overworked Mum lies about where I was hanging out on the days I should be at school. They pretended to be the deputy headmaster, a police officer or even a pimp. This was during the period that Mum and Dad were having constant meetings with form tutors, school attendance officers, employment agencies, concerned family members, concerned friends, concerned parents of friends and employers and officers and finally youth welfare and the local crime prevention scheme. I've bashed and kicked to pieces so many bikes and lockers and maize stalks and windows of deserted barns in the countryside. I've missed so many lessons. There were constant negotiations, there were constant struggles, there were constant changes in strategy, there was no break. There was no time to recover from the screaming. This is Year 9. This is the fighting spanning three whole years.

And the clock, which, in its own time, stretched this season of bad news and bad things with every fucking second, ignored my cycle rides through the maize and strawberry and cabbage fields, the meadows with the cows and the garden centre turf that was cut out on Sundays to be sold, ignored those rides that I made more than anything else because I hoped somehow that when I got home afterwards, sweaty and exhausted, the situation might have changed, that this day or the next, after my cycling into the ticking of time, had caused that clock to behave like it had before, before all this, before the bad news, the bad things, the screaming. I cycled without mobile or watch, alone along the boggy, brown meadow, into the ticking of time. I cycled until I was dizzy and sick. Of course I don't feel guilty. How can I possibly feel guilty? I didn't moan and I worked hard and then I realised it did me no fucking good whatsoever.

MY FIRST TEMPORARY RELEASE DAY falls on a Wednesday. I'm allowed to go to the library in town, with Savanna. Although it's been three months since I stepped inside this building, I know exactly how to show my laminated pass to the security guard, which gates we have to go through, how long we have to wait until one door closes and the other one opens again. I should look forward to it, but guess what.

Savanna leads me to the gates and when the big front door of the detention centre falls shut behind us, I look up, to the overcast spring sky. Together we leave the grounds. Although Savanna suggests we take the bus, I want to walk to the library. It takes us half an hour before we're there and I try to enjoy the freedom I feel in the muscles of my upper legs. We cross the residential area and then make our way towards the centre. It feels as if people are gazing at me, even though I'm sad and I'm looking down, at the paving stones on which my worn-out trainers are treading, instead of at the people. I think: Can they see it in me?

Savanna walks next to me and then behind me and directs whether we should go left or right, where we cross the road.

'We're very proud of you, of how you've developed,' she says. 'How you have grown.'

I sneeze because the pollen tickles my nose and say thank you. An old woman on a bike takes a bend very slowly and I'd so love to sit on a saddle and ride along the canal outside the village until I get to the point where it runs into the river.

When we get to the library I have a cig first.

'Are you looking forward to this?' Savanna asks.

'Yes,' I reply. 'Massively.'

Marissa told me that on her first time she had to really hold herself back not to jump on the first bus and make a run for it.

However much I was looking forward to this day, since Marissa fought with the supervisors and with her leaving date inching closer, this whole outing leaves me entirely cold. Something's very, very broken.

We enter the library and it's quiet, in that lovely way I remember from the past, when Miriam and I went on Saturdays with Mum, and eventually on my own. First the reading desks and magazine racks, then the rows and rows of books. Children's books, thrillers, archaeology, translated books, English. I don't even know which titles I want to pick up. I see a few copies of *Little Crumb*, the children's book about the abandoned boy who has to earn his keep in the streets before he's allowed back home again. In the poetry section a thin volume stands by itself on the shelf, its cover facing me. Vasalis. I think Mum has something by Vasalis. I pick it up and leaf through the poems. Savanna leans against one of the bookcases and observes me, as if I'm an actor and she my audience. I move on and look at the covers with empty cots, silhouettes in the street, dancing people, paintings, enormous screaming letters or very ornate ones, photos of landscapes, birds, lambs. I stop at a book with a bunch of cows and a cloudy sky as its cover. *The Twin*, it says.

A woman goes over to the desk to the right of Savanna and me and whispers a question to the man sitting there. He answers in full voice.

'That's in Philosophy, at the back.' He points. My fingers glide along the covers. Although I've read everything that Mum has brought for me, everything for lack of choice, I now don't know. Savanna leafs through a book with pictures of nature reserves, and keeps an eye on me.

'Is there nothing that you want to read?' she asks, and I shake my head. I should choose a book, and be excited about that. This term, in Greek, we were going to translate a section from the *Iliad*: 'Sing, Goddess, the son of Peleus Achilles' rage,' it said on the first page of the textbook.

The rest of the hour we traipse past the shelves. My hands refuse to pick up anything. This is the end of something, that's how it feels. It's ugly and doesn't stop, it's all dying so slowly. I don't want words. Maybe another Salomé would, or on another day, but now I don't want them.

Savanna places her hand on my shoulder when she finds me somewhere near a shelf with history books.

'We're going in a minute.'

I'm allowed to go to the loo first and while I'm sitting on the bowl I rest my head in my hands. Before I flush I look down and between the pee and the toilet paper floats clear, red blood. I pull more loo paper from the roll and stuff it into my knickers.

Shortly afterwards we leave the library. Savanna asks if I had a nice time.

'No,' I say, and then, after a brief silence: 'I've got my period.'

'Oh, sweetie,' says Savanna in a tone I've not heard from her before.

We wait for the traffic light to cross and then she takes me to a chemist's just outside the centre. Inside the light's blazing, white. It smells of soap and powder and the perfume bottles behind glass.

'Sanitary towels or tampons?' she asks, but all I can do is cry like an idiot. She bangs packages in her basket, grabs two boxes of paracetamol from another shelf and pulls me by the arm to the till. She pays for the box of tampons, together with the own-brand sanitary towels with wings, and the paracetamol. She also buys a bar of chocolate and puts it all in her bag.

'It'll be all right,' she says.

'I just want it to stop,' I say.

'You're doing so well, really.'

We walk back. I bite my cheek to stop crying, but it doesn't work. My belly begins to ache. With the water from her bottle I swallow three paracetamol as we're waiting for the red light.

'Would you like some chocolate?' Savanna asks.

'No,' I snap.

When we're back in the Donut I go straight to my room. Savanna watches me, how I keep turning right interminably. I know this because I look behind me. I see how she stares at me moving away, with her hands in her trouser pockets.

MARISSA'S DRUG TEST WAS POSITIVE and she had to talk to Frits and the director and her lip was swollen. So that's what she meant in the laundry room when she said she'd got what she wanted after the boys' riot.

Her swollen lip didn't feature in the meeting with the director. All being well she'll still be allowed to go home next week, she told me in the bathroom.

'They just want shot of me.' Her chin's barely purple now after the wrestling and her fall. The cut next to her eyebrow, near the star at the end of the curly letters ONELUV, is hardly visible either. I moved my hand to her chin, rested it on the discoloured skin.

'Sorry I didn't help,' I said. Her skin was soft, it startled me.

'I didn't expect you to,' she said, taking my wrist and pulling my hand down. 'It doesn't hurt.'

She's been quiet over the past few days. Silent. I think she did it on purpose. She told me about her family. Her brother, her elder sister, her mother and aunt. The places she used to go to in Eindhoven, the people she knew and who she was or wasn't afraid of. How often she saw her father.

When Marissa talks about her family, I get the feeling she knows exactly where she stands with everyone. That she understands them and they understand her, even though they're all completely crazy: 'difficult'. She talks about them with love, has said they're all going to pick her up together. Even her father. I wonder how my family talks about me, to others. Whether they've already arranged who'll drive the car here. Who will make the journey. My stomach ache's gone, but during dinner I can't get anything down. I'm cold. I'm shivering.

MARCO COMES TO TAKE MY TEMPERATURE and says I should stay in bed.

'I'll come and see how you're doing in an hour or two,' he says. He disappears and I can only just about turn over. I feel blood pour out of me, down my full sanitary towel and leg. There's a big stain on my bottom sheet, but it leaves me cold just now.

I dream about a sea that smashes its waves against the rocks and wake up fall asleep wake up fall asleep, take a painkiller and press my nose into the pillow.

My room smells of waste and fever and I'm half asleep and I dream. In my dream I slowly and wearily tidy up my clothes and things that are lying about, I make my bed disappear, my loo, my cupboard I push into the wall until it's gone, until the room's completely empty, empty and white and just me there in the middle, and then I zip open my stomach and remove all my innards, I push these through the wall as well, flush my brains down the loo, I slowly fold up my skin, give my eyes to the crows, bury my hands, below ground, all I am is a lump of flesh, my torso with four protrusions. Eliminated. Neat.

WHEN I USED TO BASH DAD'S PUNCHBALL in the garage there was always music playing, but this is something no one told me: fighting is very silent. As if the public's waiting for an orchestra, but the orchestra's nervous, keeps dropping its instruments, the music's then the sound of the dropping instruments. Sometimes an *ah* resounds when a drum slips through someone's fingers, sometimes an off-key note from the trumpet, a brief shriek.

I'm not actually all that strong. I fought because of all the bad things. The season of the bad things, the bad news.

In Greek tragedies a bad thing never happens in isolation. It's foretold by a messenger and everyone knows from the outset how the play will unfold. It's always this plus this plus this like a wave, a current, whole generations cursed, caught in destinies. They don't need to be like this but they don't know any better. Just think about it, said Mrs Doormans, all that tragedy!

It keeps on blooming, bubbling up, blowing with full force. It keeps on yanking branches from trees and collapsing the roofs of houses. It screeches. It bleeds. Just like then.

On 18 October 2007, a year after Dad was sacked last winter, this winter, when the clock's ticking became so loud that it stopped me from sleeping, Salvatore and Paul followed me on my bike home and cornered me. It was cold and on the road in the distance the cars shot past while I was cycling from school to the village, and when I looked back I saw them racing towards me like hounds. I was bait. They overtook me. They pushed and they pulled.

It could've been other boys.

It could've been girls.

It could've been Teun or Gijs or Chantal or Irene or Sofie. It was this plus this plus this. It could've gone differently, but I didn't know any better. I was too busy.

I kicked them off me. Salvatore tall and lanky, Paul a little rat. They grabbed my coat and hung on to me until I fell off my bike. It's quite a boring story, actually. Have you ever tried explaining a fight scene from a film? *Die Hard with a Vengeance* without the one-liners and with the sound off. You end up talking about bodies flying around in an abandoned warehouse and paralysed limbs, guns without a bang.

The field was a kilometre wide and endlessly long. The sheep were on the other side of the road, and the cows huddled together in a group. The field, left unattended, was waiting. The field was waiting for me, I had cycled around it time and again, mustering up courage to go to school, but it was only then that I understood. The grass was green and wet with cold and it was waiting. The boys were waiting. They were cursing and they were waiting. And I scrambled up from the cycle path, my hip throbbing with pain, a graze on the palm of the hand with which I caught my fall. It didn't have to be this way, but I simply tumbled into it.

I looked at Salvatore and shouted: 'What did you say to me, you fucking piece of fucking shit?'

Tick. Tick. Tick. Tick. Tick.

Their statement would later say: 'Beside herself with anger.'

They called it 'a superhuman strength'. She's 'extremely *intimidating*'. She's 'cruel'. Nothing was said about how it sounded. The laughter. How it sounded when I fell into the cold water. Into the sludge.

And of course it happened quickly; I sometimes cross the line with how I talk about things, but now I'm choosing my words very carefully, because of course it happened quickly and it hurt.

Everything so clear.

I was lying in the ditch, with my head above the water. My clothes sucking up water until they were saturated, dragging me down. I wanted to stay there and sink to the bottom of the silence of this dirty, dirty ditch. But I also wanted something else, something unknown.

'Look at her lying there!' Salvatore laughed, getting his phone from his pocket and taking a picture. I stared at the sky and thought of my books sucking up all that water, ink letters turning into big, black drops and dissolving in the sludge.

How I would look in the picture, glistening from the mud and my hair floating between the algae. Medusa. Look at me and I turn you to stone. Tick. Tick. Tick.

'Out you get, out you get!'

I scrambled up, yes, scrambled to my feet, and clambered out of the ditch, yes, first my bag on the edge of the bank and then myself and they were laughing and laughing and the grass the water the mud in my hands, and as I was crawling over the ground between the ditch and the bike path, I grabbed the first thing I could find, the first thing was my bike, and I pulled my bike out of the water, my bike suddenly so light in my mud my grass my hands, and Salvatore laughed and spat on the ground and Paul kicked my bag away and that dull wet thud

and I pulled the bike I pulled the bike with all my might I swung the bike I swung it backwards with all my might lifted it with all my might and swung it and gravity did its work those are two kinds of force

all I needed to do was give the way forward an extra push gravity helped to propel those two kinds of force forwards the steel the wheels the handlebars with all that might those two kinds of force into Salvatore's stomach with rubber steel plastic panels

collapsing backwards onto the red path tarmac and Paul running towards me dirty fucking whore and I jumped over the ditch catch me then if you can with my heavy shield of wet clothes incest bitch catch me then into the meadow but he was quick and caught me

and the small firm body on top of my big firm body

with two forces two kinds of force in the cowpat like a dance

the fighting in the mud and the shit doesn't make any noise it's just nails knees and shit algae teeth hair the bleeding and the flesh but most important of all when the other joined him and they began kicking me and me on my side and them on top of me spitting and walking away as if job done I thought no

motherfuckers no

because I had blood in my mouth the blood between my teeth and that's when with the iron and the blood and the fists I got the taste the force the wind's cold and I have a stick in my hand I see everything clearly the distances the colours and how everything is connected.

You must take a step forward for every jab, said Dad, as if you're punching right through the enemy.

They're a mouth and a fist and they are kissing.

It's delicious.

I'm happy and awake and I see everything. It's light and cold and I'm awake the screeching. I'm in the world I'm naked in the desert I'm extremely light I'm awake I screech with elbows swimming in flesh.

I don't creep up on anyone, but the fight's silent. Nothing is silent like three bodies colliding in a field at the edge of the B-road and with blood in my mouth I look for and find the body of the other while cars and tractors and trucks whizz past.

When I run home, I can still hear the banging and the jeering. The light along the motorway's blazing. The world's white but wants her colours back. And while I'm running I beg, but she won't take no for an answer. She wants red and brown and green and black, because it's already getting dark.

She wants red in the dark. She wants blue and black. She wants yellow like lamp posts. She wants it to make a sound. For the sound to be pure. For it to be as sharply honed as a sword.

She wants to hear it and she wants it now.

'YOU'VE SLEPT A LONG TIME,' says Zainab when I get to the common room. 'The doctor even came to see you.'

'Where's Marissa?' I ask. The fluorescent light hurts my eyes. My skull feels too small for my brain. There's dried menstrual blood stuck underneath my fingernails and I can't get rid of it.

'Gone out again. Wanna sit?'

'It's okay,' I say. 'Can I make a call in a minute? Where's Savanna?'

'Are you sure? Shouldn't you be going back to bed?'

It makes no difference. It isn't me anyway.

I say no. No, I don't want to. I want to call home, dammit.

I cry like a baby till they unlock the door of the phone room.

Mum answers straight away.

'How are you?'

'Better.'

'Do you still have a temperature?'

'Almost gone.'

'Great,' she says, 'I was getting worried. How was your day out? How was the library?'

'Not now,' I say and then I sigh. 'I mean, fine.'

'What did you read?' Miriam's voice asks.

'Is Dad around?'

'Here I am.'

'Nothing,' I say.

'What do you mean, nothing?'

'Mum, Dad. I want to go home.'

Not a sound. I take a sip of water. I take another sip of water, and with the receiver wedged between my shoulder and ear, pick the blood from underneath my nails. My sheets still haven't been washed.

'As a child, when you felt out of sorts, you'd also get ill,' Dad says. He sounds nostalgic, like when we reminisce about our holidays in Zeeland. How Miriam burnt her ankles on the beach.

'That's not true,' I say, like a child.

There's laughter. I clutch the phone. I want it to be here. For the laughter to be here.

No. It's not true. I want to be there and hear it all without interference.

'Oh yes it is,' Miriam says in a teasing tone of voice, warm, and I start to cry, very loudly. It comes from very deep within me.

MARISSA GIVES ME A HUG. We're sitting inside, on the common room's leather sofa. The others are outside, where it's less hot than in here, with the sun beating down on the venetian blinds. Our bare knees are touching each other and I can feel our skins sticking. I no longer have a temperature, but am still snivelling. Marissa says it's all the same to her. She's wearing her gold chain over her tank top and the tag with BADBITCH chafes my neck when she lets go of me.

'Will you come and see me?'

'Yes,' I say.

'I'll call you and then I'll give you my number, than we can ping when you're out.'

'I don't have a BlackBerry, you dope,' I say. Some time tomorrow morning Marissa will be collected by her elder sister, her mother, her father and her aunt.

'Don't let them fuck you around, right?' she says.

I nod. She thumps my shoulder.

'Hey,' she says. 'I mean it.'

'Yeah yeah.'

'When you come and see me we'll have a McDonald's first and then go and see a movie. A good movie.' She grins.

'I don't know what's on at the moment.'

'I choose. No romcom bullshit. The new *Batman*'s coming out soon, innit?'

'We'll see, man,' I say, and sniff. Marissa looks away. I look at my hands. The layer of cold sweat in the palms of my hands, which has been there since this morning. I'm glad Marissa's going, for her. In the end you have to wrap it up all by yourself. There's a small heart on her right-hand index finger; on her middle, ring and little finger the number 040. Blue ink. A slight bulge on the skin. I want to stroke it with my thumb.

'You're going to come, right?' she then says with a trembling voice.

'Hey,' I say, but she shakes her head and gets up, wipes her face with her forearm.

'Whatever. I'm going out, are you coming?'

'Listen—'

'Just come.'

I don't move for a while, but then she clicks her tongue and goes over to the door. I follow her. Outside we lean against the fence in the corner of the yard. Marissa says nothing. Spring's loud and disgusting. I start to sweat even more, as if I've got another temperature, as if I need to go back to bed. The girls are spread out across the tarmac, bored. Everyone's wearing shorts, apart from Feline, who's wearing a skirt. Everyone has bare arms. Geert and Savanna are having a smoke together. If I think away the fences which I know are behind the building, it could easily be a school playground.

I take Marissa's hand. Briefly. And I take a step closer to her. She says nothing, just looks at me from the corner of her eye. She's a little bit taller than me. I thought she was a lot taller in fact. Our hips collide and then I let go. She wriggles her hand between the fence and my lower back. The palm of her hand feels warm through the fabric of my shirt.

'Game of basketball, Salomé?'

'No, don't feel like it,' I say.

'You never fucking feel like anything.'

'Yeah yeah.'

She pulls back her arm. We both raise a foot, place our soles against the concrete of the wall. I lift my head towards the sun, eyes closed. It glows orange through my lashes, my eyelids.

WHEN I WAKE UP the next morning she's gone. The runny nose's gone, the temperature's gone, Marissa's gone. I pull the sheets from the bed and turn over the bloody mattress.

At breakfast I'm sitting alone, with a chair between Zainab and me. I don't want to fucking talk. Not with anyone. In bed I've done a lot of thinking, about time. How it drags and how quickly it can go. How it moves between events.

A time frame's an interval between moments, the time between one event and another. That's what it more or less says in my dictionary. How much time was there between Dad losing his job and my sentence? How much time between when Marissa said yo, with that look, and the first time she did my hair? How much time between shoving someone off their bike and that person picking up a stick, starting to beat you up? You have to get really close and pay attention if you want to catch time. You have to pay attention and catch it.

No one's turning his motherfucking back to me, I screamed with blood in my mouth, so that's the moment I grabbed him, that I looked around and hooked him with my clutches, my answer was the ticking of the time I needed to grab hold of him, I grabbed the big, black, long, fat stick. I took my time, let myself go until time had run out.

Here it feels different. Here you can keep on clutching but there's no grip. I don't think we need to talk about it much longer. That there's any need for that. I've got the picture. Now that Marissa's gone all the other stuff doesn't really matter. The visits, the phone calls, the girls who run away and are brought back, who are transferred, get released, get qualifications, will never see boyfriends again, who cry, cry cry cry, who are replaced and disappear themselves, exchanged, temporary release, fucking lesbo, *rehabilitation*, blah blah blah. It's all part of the waiting. It happens between events. It's white noise. It's tacky.

NOW THAT I'M ALONE, THE fun's gone somewhat. Because I keep my trap shut the whole time, they think I'm making progress, that I'm on the right track. I'm doing my time.

Waiting means taking the poison every day and smiling. Eight of us being shoved into a minibus to tidy up a park. Watch how Zainab finally flips and smashes Ashli in the face. More temporary release. Zainab crying in isolation. Smashing plates because plates are being hurled at you and spending the whole day in your room a couple of times because you were mean to the new supervisor but also make up with him and again someone escapes, is brought back, and so it continues. Waiting waiting waiting and the preparation for release and then all of a sudden not wanting to go. While I'm preparing to go home Ashli leaves and a new girl comes along and does all the things we've done. It's nothing new. It's boring.

The second time I'm on temporary release I'm allowed to go home. The fourth time I'm allowed to stay the night. I sit next to Mum on the sofa and watch TV all day. We eat rice with chicken, and those custard buns I like, and I tell Mum that I'm sorry when she comes to wish me goodnight, when I lie in my own bed, in my own room.

Be powerful, step forward with your jab. That was the goal. It doesn't feel as I expected it would.

'It'll all be all right,' says Mum.

I don't sleep that night. Miriam isn't there for breakfast.

The cooking, taking a test and getting an A for it and not feeling anything, the smoking smoking smoking smoking smoking waiting waiting smoking and Frits.

'It's going well,' he tells me when I speak with him again. 'Don't you think?'

147

I look at him. At the map. The hole punch. The photo of his stupid shitty dog.

'Yes, brilliantly,' I say.

'Do you think you might be ready to share with the group how you ended up here?'

Ashli's done this. Feline. Marissa. You have to stand in front of the group and reveal everything. In films this is the big dénouement, you discover something, weight off your shoulders. Blah blah blah.

'I don't want to,' I say.

'I think it'll do you good,' he says. 'As soon as you can talk about it—'

'I don't want to talk about it,' I snap. 'It's no use to anyone and doesn't help me either.'

'It's just part of the process.'

'Others can do that to make themselves feel special,' I say.

'Special?' Frits frowns and stares out of the window angrily. 'What makes you think that? Why do you always have to be contrary at the wrong moments?'

'Because you always think at the wrong moment that you know how I tick.'

When I'm ready we have to go to the common room, stand in line. Henny isn't there. Her sentence was reduced on appeal and she's officially done her time now. When she came to tell me I gave her a fist-bump, but she was in a state of panic. She had twenty-four hours to pack her things. They chucked her out onto the street after breakfast with a bin bag full of clothes.

Positioned between Savanna and Geert a new girl's waiting for us. She's crying. She's shaking all over. Zainab yawns. It's all the same. They come, they go, they appear and disappear, they aren't anything, nor am I.

'This is Sharon,' says Savanna.

She doesn't raise her hand and nor do we.

FRITS IS OFF ON HOLIDAY, the last two weeks that I'm here. 'Trekking in South Africa, on the motorbike,' I hear him tell Marco. I roll my eyes. Everyone who won't see him again after his holiday gets a card. Mine has a giraffe on it, Kyara an elephant. The new one has a pony. In all our three cards it says in Frits's writing BEST OF LUCK WITH YOUR FUTURE. I fling the thing straight in the bin, squeeze toothpaste onto it. The temporary therapist introduces herself the next morning at breakfast. Our sessions are a complete waste of time, are about nothing, are short. But then the sun is rising as well, earlier and earlier, the last warmth of spring. Marco who brings along rocket ice lollies at the weekend and Zainab who has her hair cut. How her eyes shine all of a sudden, how quickly the summer arrives.

FROM DAD'S SHOULDERS I SAW the market in the centre of Douala, that time in Cameroon. Standing on the hill that looked out onto a street market, below us a sea of cloths spread out, an incomprehensible pattern stretched across ropes and poles, hanging from which were fish and fabrics, beads, hats, CDs and plastic artifacts. Some stalls had a roof of drying herbs, others, parasols attached to the corners of carts on which corn and peanuts were roasted. Sometimes I thought I was looking at the fabric of a stall, but this turned out to be the heads of people who were pushing their way through the traders, talking loudly or kicking at stray dogs and chickens.

That's how I remember it in any case. Later Dad said that the market we went to wasn't really all that busy.

'Beautiful, isn't it?' Dad asked on that hill, avoiding a moped that shot past us. The car was parked a few hundred metres away.

'Yes,' I replied, with my hands in his hair, 'yes, yes, yes.' Looking out over the market's narrow alleys, sitting on Dad's shoulders, I yearned to have all the silver watches from all the dead grandmas on my wrist so that I could wave at all the market traders like a glittering princess.

I'd never felt as hot as on that day in the city. Dad had taken me to meet an old schoolfriend. We took the short route, down the hill, through the market street. Dad carried me on his head, like the fruit baskets that were balanced on the heads of some of the women. We stopped at a stall where Dad and his friend were going to eat fish. I can remember this clearly because of the six or so umbrellas that had been tied together to protect customers against the sun. The umbrellas were held aloft with wooden poles and ropes above two plastic tables, with upturned crates to sit on. The strung-together umbrellas cast diamond-shaped dark grey shadows on the amber sand across which businessmen, school pupils and women with fully laden bags trudged. Dad and his friend talked fast in Ewondo. He'd put me on his knee with one hand, while using the other to smoke and eat. I sweated and sweated, it ran into my eczema spots, drips trickled into my eyes, and Dad wiped both our faces every so often with a dirty napkin. I was happy and allowed the friend to pinch my cheek and I played Snake on Dad's phone while mimicking the incomprehensible words, how Dad's voice sank deeper and buzzed. The market's and the seagulls' screeching, the din of the cars, the vapours, the heat, when I think of that now, it seems as if the entire holiday with my family concentrated around that, that moment with Dad on the side of a dusty road.

Miriam and Mum were at home in bed with food poisoning. Aunt Céleste had joked a bit at first.

'Are you pretending my food makes you ill?' she'd asked with raised eyebrows, but for two nights now Miriam had been legging it out of our room every half hour to get to the loo as fast as she could, where, groaning, she'd empty her stomach. It was the water, it was the heat, it was the pre-packaged doughnuts we'd bought en route into town from a street vendor who scuttled up and down between stationary cars on the side of the road with a basket full of bottled water and snacks.

A boy in a big, ripped shirt positioned himself next to us. I looked at the grey-green ragged shirt that he was wearing over a pair of sandals that looked like they'd been carved from car tyres. When Dad waved him away the boy pulled a funny face at me and I stuck out my tongue. Then he slogged on. Dad and his childhood friend laughed and I grinned back, through the stars I kept seeing in front of my eyes as a result of the heat.

During the long journey back to the family home I fell asleep in the back of the car. I shivered when I woke up and went straight back inside, exhausted, to lie down on the sofa next to Uncle Honoré, who was watching TV. I didn't wake up until dinner time. During dinner I suddenly became very despondent. I looked at my family, the food on the table, the hands reaching for dishes, the oilcloth. It all looked so sad, so far away. The house so white and big and cool, the sun shining so fiercely, everywhere smelling of dried tree leaves and petrol, everyone I met in the street trudging en route to the village or town, the fruit being colourful, the village church always full, the old folk sleeping on the veranda, the fact that there was always someone in and around the house. The goat we wound up. The soup simmering for hours. The radio that was always on. The TV with its bad reception. I'd only seen the sea from a distance, from the car, but I was already missing that as well.

The day we went home Mum was sitting at the dinner table with a contorted face drinking a cup of bouillon. Miriam was still asleep in our room.

'Are you ready to go home?' she asked, and I burst into tears.

I can't remember how we said goodbye to the family, but I do remember that it felt as if it was impossible. That I thought: How can I go back to the Netherlands after I've seen this? Aunt Céleste gave us big hugs. Uncle Honoré shook my hand. Antoine said, 'Until next time,' in his cute Dutch.

Dad put me in Uncle Jacques' car where I leaned against Mum and inhaled her sickly, nauseous smell. En route to the airport the car had to stop three times so that Mum and Miriam could let their diarrhoea run free behind the shrubs along the motorway.

'I'm done, I'm done,' Miriam wailed.

'Next time you come it won't be so bad,' Uncle Jacques said. He made a joke about Westerners I didn't get then. I was sitting with my legs resting on a bag with damp cloths and loo paper that was yanked from underneath my feet every so often, so that Miriam or Mum could wipe their bums. There was whining. Dad and Uncle Jacques said nothing or cursed the traffic. I didn't even have the energy to cry.

In the car it was baking hot. The uncomfortable feeling of saying goodbye to my family had turned into stomach ache and this stomach ache gave me cold shivers, and because of the fever I can only remember how I was moved from shoulder to chest like a rag doll when we got to the airport, slumping against Mum's breast and sitting on Dad's knee while we waited at the gate. During the flight I also got diarrhoea.

'Not you as well now?' Dad grumbled when I crawled back into my seat having spent fifteen minutes on the loo. The stewardess emptied a sachet of Imodium and minerals into my lukewarm tea and Mum placed the paper cup to my lips until I had drunk it all. Miriam had been asleep for some time.

In the middle of the night we transferred in Istanbul, and at the end of the afternoon we arrived in Brussels. I ate a cheese roll while Mum went to get the car.

'We have to walk a bit,' said Dad. 'Can you do that?'

I nodded and began to get up but didn't feel my feet touch the ground. When I'd lifted my full weight off the chair I simply collapsed on the airport's floor tiles. I can still hear Dad's scream. A few hours later we drove past the Welcome to the Netherlands sign on the motorway.

WHEN I OPEN THE DOOR to Miriam's room, it smells of perfume and old beer, just like yesterday and the day before and the day before that. Her black hair with blonde plaits sticks out above the sheet she pulled over her head. Boxes full of packed stuff are stacked under the attic window; the harsh summer sunlight shines through the gaps of the blinds. She snores.

'Dad says you need to get up,' I say loudly. She starts, then drops her head back into the pillow, groans. I lean against the door frame with my shoulder. Miriam throws off the sheet. Her body's drenched in sweat. The white shirt she's wearing sticks against her stomach. She puts her hand on her forehead and around her wrist are the silver bracelets she always wears.

'What time is it?'

'Half eleven or something.'

'Fuck. Where are Mum and Dad?' She rummages for her phone. I hear the pigeons on the roof, their flapping wings, their legs shuffling through the leaves and the muck on the roof tiles.

'Mum's getting dressed. Dad's in the garage,' I say.

'My head, man.' She turns over slowly, sits on the edge of the bed and takes the glass of water next to it, drinks it in one swig.

'Was it fun last night?' I ask.

'Yeah. Not too busy.'

Mum came to collect me from the Donut two weeks ago, at ten a.m. I'd hardly slept, and since breakfast had been sitting on the bed with all my packed stuff next to me waiting for Marco. He came to get me at five to nine, took me to the reception area.

I had to hand in my laminated pass. I don't know if it felt good. It happened very quickly. Somewhere in the Donut is my file. They still have my fingerprints.

Miriam gets up from the bed, goes over to the window and

154

pulls up the blind. The bright sunlight crashes into the attic room.

'Jesus,' she grumbles.

The second day I was at home Miriam and I both had to go shopping in town with Mum. It was boiling hot. Mum went inside and we waited in the car in the car park with the doors open. Miriam was smoking cigs with her feet outside, angry because she couldn't go and see her friends.

'Fucking bullshit,' she said.

'What?' I asked.

'My whole afternoon ruined, yeah?'

'What can I do about that?'

She looked at me through the window of the car door.

'Oh, this ain't your fault then?'

I already had a headache. I opened the back door and stood in front of her, bent over. Miriam gazing up with raised eyebrows.

'What do you want from me?' I shouted.

'Give me those shorts,' she says now. Miriam points at the cane chair next to the door with some blue exercise shorts on it. On the back of them it says IBIZA in fat white letters. I grab the shorts, throw them onto the bed.

'I don't need to help as well, right?' she says, getting up and hoisting her legs into the shorts. 'I really won't make it.'

I shrug my shoulders and turn around, go downstairs.

I hear Mum fiddling around in her bedroom. The smell of the Scented Rose shower gel she's washed herself with lingers in the corridor.

Miriam, two weeks ago, pushed herself up from the car seat and flicked her cigarette into the bushes where the nose of the car was parked.

'What are you going to do?' she said. 'Hit me? Is this supposed to scare me?'

I go down the stairs, through the hallway, the kitchen, the utility room, to the garage where Dad, cigarette between his lips. is standing in front of the shelving unit with the tools.

'Miriam's awake,' I say. Dad turns towards me.

'Put this in that box,' he says. He points with a hammer and two screwdrivers at the toolbox. I slog towards him through the piles of junk, take the hammer and screwdrivers from his hand.

When Mum came out of the supermarket, with four big bags in the shopping trolley and a red face, I went up to her on my own to help her.

'What happened?' she asked. I said nothing. I'd already wiped Miriam's spit from my cheek.

When Mum came to pick me up from the Donut we drove home past the farm fields. They were in a parched state in the fierce August sun. Mum had rested her right hand on my knee. She only removed it every so often to change gears, as if she was afraid I'd jump out of the car. Once home, Miriam greeted me in the hall with her slim arms and glittering eye make-up. She slowly pulled me towards her, as if she had to hug a frail old dear, and said: 'So.'

So.

In the car park she shouted: 'Get lost, moron.'

In two weeks' time Miriam's moving to the Laak quarter in The Hague where she's going to study International Business Management at college. During the journey home from the Donut, when Mum didn't want to remove her hand from my knee, she said she didn't understand, she really didn't understand, why Miriam insisted on doing a degree course that didn't suit her one bit.

'It's as if she threw a dart at the course prospectus,' she said.

She also said that she hoped, really hoped, that it would mean the end of her relationship with her boyfriend Jeffrey.

'What an out and out dork.'

When I got home my whole family was still there. My room, my bed, the books in the bookcase, the TV, the cutlery in the cutlery drawer. They're all still there.

'Why can you never just be my sister,' I shouted, 'instead of acting as if I'm a fucking fly, you fucking selfish piece of turd?'

That's when she spat in my face.

We're getting the things together for Miriam's new room: crockery, dining chairs, kitchen utensils, stored in the garage, all from the house in Breskens where Grandma and Grandpa had lived for just a year when they both, within two months of each other, died. Grandpa from a heart attack, Grandma from grief. That's what Mum always says.

I put the tools in the black box with a tray of nails, a tray of screws and a drill.

'Where's your sister?'

'Having a shower, I think.'

Dad goes over to the radio and pauses the tape with rumba, twiddles some knobs until we hear the news on Sky Radio. It's baking hot in the garage, even with the door open and the old fan blowing. There are pearls of sweat in Dad's neck and, despite having put on a clean shirt, I smell my own sweat.

'Are you going to see Lili?'

'I don't know yet,' I reply. Each time I want to ring Liliana, I'm overcome by despondency.

'Are you staying out of trouble? That girl is . . .' He waves with his hand and opens a box in the corner of the garage.

Mum comes into the garage, smelling of deodorant and the stuff she always puts in her hair. She's combed her short, wet hair back and is wearing a loose dress, which falls over her round upper legs like a tent.

'Have you found my mother's crockery?' she asks, with her hands on her hips.

'Gone,' says Dad.

'You should look at what it says on the boxes.'

Dad dumps the opened box on the workbench and takes his cigarettes from his trouser pocket.

'It probably says Breskens or something. Or Grandpa and Grandma.'

'Everything says Breskens,' he carps, 'or Grandpa and Grandma. Look for it yourself.'

Mum begins to lift the stacked boxes one by one, to read the labels she stuck on them when we had to empty the house.

'Salomé, go upstairs and tell Miriam not to go out until she's had a look at Grandma's curtains.'

'Why would she want that old-bag-junk?' Dad grumbles. 'And

why can your daughter go wherever she likes while we sort out her move?'

I close the black toolbox.

'Get your sister,' Mum says, and places one of the removal boxes on the bench. It makes the sound of crashing crockery. Dad turns up the radio. I leave the garage, climb the stairs again.

Miriam swears when I find her in the bathroom. She's just put on her make-up. Her plaits are gathered in a tail on her head.

'I don't need any fucking granny curtains,' she says, following me down the stairs.

'Why don't you just tell them?'

She sighs. When we get to the kitchen, the fridge hums.

'What's the atmosphere like there, anyway?' Instead of following me into the garage Miriam opens one of the kitchen cabinets and grabs a glass, goes over to the sink and lets the tap run. She feels the spout with her extended finger. The fridge makes a plopping sound. The humming's turning into a kind of gurgling, as if the compressor's switching off. Then it falls silent.

'The atmosphere?' I ask.

'In the garage,' she says. She fills the glass with cold water and turns off the tap.

'The longer you kick your heels, the worse, in any case.'

'Whatever.'

'Just come along.'

'Calm down, bitch.' Miriam opens the fridge door, roots with her fingers in an open packet of cooked chicken, pulls out a slice and drops the meat into her mouth. The fridge starts to hum again. The fridge had been Grandma and Grandpa's. It's been here for five years or so, I think.

I can do without this on top of everything else, said Mum driving out of the car park. The shopping crashed into the side of the boot as she took the bend.

Please, both of you, she said.

Please.

'Are you coming?' I ask, massaging my temples with both hands.

'Is there something you have to do?' Miriam takes another slice of chicken, wraps it around her middle finger, pushes it into her mouth. Then she shuts the fridge door.

When we get to the garage, Dad's smoking a cigarette on the workbench stool while he's counting a bunch of metal rings from a plastic bag. Mum's set out plates and bowls.

'Here, look,' she says to Miriam, pointing at the white plates. 'And also have a look at Grandma's curtains.'

'Can't I get new ones?'

Dad grins at Mum, who sticks her middle finger up at him. She combs her hands through her drying hair. It shines. A little tuft behind her left ear's got tangled.

'We have to go to The Hague next Wednesday. Are you going to order curtains before then? We don't even know the measurements of the room.'

'You can have my curtains,' I say.

'What a crap idea,' replies Miriam. She's picked up Grandma's floral curtains, holds the fabric between her thumb and index finger. 'Plus, you'll end up sleeping without.'

'I could move to the attic?'

'That's my room!'

'You just take Grandma's curtains and when we have the money for new ones, we buy them.' Mum lifts a breakfast plate from a box with two hands, almost as an apology, and gives it to Miriam. 'And?'

'Yes, fine.' Miriam drops the curtain onto the garage floor, puts the plate back in the box. 'Can I go see Carlita and Alexandra in a minute?'

'No,' says Dad. He beckons me. 'Do you want me to keep this?' He points at the punchball, which is standing behind the fishing rods, next to the wall with his tools on it.

'No,' I say.

'Are you sure?'

'Just put it on eBay.'

A long sceptical look. Dad rubs the leather with his big hand, pulls back his arm, makes a fist, and hits the punchball hard and fast.

'I've got a headache,' I say, to no one in particular.

'We're nearly done,' says Mum.

Dad was sitting at the dining table when I came home. He got up, walked over to me and gave me a hug.

'Welcome home,' he said. He smelt of medication and tobacco. Of cologne. Of my sick father.

'I'll be back in time,' says Miriam. 'For the rest.'

'I said no,' says Dad.

'Take a look at those stools over there,' says Mum. 'Perhaps the wood's had it, but you never know.'

I look at my family. I go over to the fan. I stand in front of it. The air that's blowing in my face is warm.

'YOU WEREN'T HERE,' Miriam had shouted. 'You were there. And I was going crazy here with Mum and Dad. While I had to do my final exams. Do you know how fucked up that is?'

I wake up at seven every morning, in keeping with the rhythm of the Donut. I get up, put on my shoes and take a walk along the canal where I rarely meet anyone at that time. I've been doing that since the first day back. After my walk I go home again, grab a bucket and a shovel and scoop up the neighbours' dog turds on the drive. I also remove the ripped bin bags from the front garden, from between the rose bushes, which have been flattened in the middle of the night or early morning.

It's been like this for two weeks or so.

The first evening I was home I heard Mum and Miriam argue in the back garden. I opened the door to the kitchen and looked through the window at them facing each other.

'It's not fair,' said Miriam. 'I also have a life.'

'It's your sister,' Mum shot back vehemently. 'She needs us now.'

'It's not only about Salomé. It's not always only about fucking Salomé.'

Other people also have a hard time.

You don't know how it comes across to me.

I got a glass from the kitchen cabinet and opened the tap to let water run into it. They didn't hear it.

'I just want to see my friends. I just want it to be normal here, just for once. For things to go the way I want them to.'

I emptied my glass in one swig. Mum stood with her hands on her hips looking up at the sky.

It's not all going smoothly. It's not as if I'd forgotten that that was never the case in my family anyway.

161

The rest of the afternoon passes with all kinds of bickering. Dad's smoking the garage blue, and Mum and Miriam are packing boxes while I go around like a dogsbody, fetching glasses of water, checking the contents of boxes, pulling extension cables out of sockets. Miriam's behaving like a princess, slouching behind Mum, whinging and saying that apart from the crockery she doesn't want anything from Grandpa and Grandma's things. At four thirty they drive to IKEA after all, for a dining table.

'If this ends up in my room,' said Miriam, when Dad and I folded out the massive, dark wooden dining table at which Grandpa and Grandma had their breakfast for centuries, 'I'll set fire to it.'

I stay with Dad in the garage. He offers me a cigarette and we smoke outside, on the plastic garden chairs.

Cigarette between his lips, he gropes in his trouser pocket and gets out his wallet. He lets his thumb run through the banknotes with squinted eyes. He fishes out a twenty euro note.

'Here,' he says.

'What?' I ask.

'You can go to the funfair.'

I take the note.

'I don't like the fair.'

'Do you want me to take it back?'

'No, no.' I fold the note up neatly and stick it in the back pocket of my denim shorts.

'You should go and do fun things. With Liliana or whoever,' says Dad, and then, after a brief silence: 'You don't need to be afraid.'

'Afraid?'

'You haven't been going outside, Salomé. Since you got home.'

'I go for a walk every day,' I say.

'You know what I mean.'

When Miriam spat in my face, I pushed her and she smashed against the boiling hot car. She screamed with pain. She called me a fucking animal and then I began to cry. I cried very loudly. I think she was embarrassed because all the shoppers were looking

162

at us. She grabbed me by the shoulders and I said sorry sorry and she said no it's fine it's all okay.

'Sometimes I really think I'm crazy,' I said, and Miriam began to laugh. 'No seriously, sometimes it's as if I don't understand what the world wants from me.'

'But you are mad,' she said. 'Man, you're just like Aunt Céleste.'

Dad's cig is nearly finished. I go to the wheelie bin, which has an empty jar of pasta sauce on it with stubbed-out butts inside. I put it between us on the ground and Dad adds his finished cigarette to the stinking filters lying in the ash.

'I don't know where to go,' I say.

'Listen,' he says, resting his hand on my neck as he blows out the smoke through his nose. 'Take it easy. Nothing's going to happen.'

I look at the blackbird flying into the big berry tree next door. It chirps and looks back and forth a bit nervously. Dad smells so different. His hair's gone so grey so quickly. The idea that he once threatened to kill the neighbours. During the six months that I've been away he's changed into an old, sick man. Just like Miriam's changed into a student. Mum into an old, tired woman. I into who I am now, whoever that is. I rest my elbows on my thighs and lean forward.

'What I say is simply true,' says Miriam. 'Everyone's completely bonkers. Everyone deals with that in a fucked up way. You and Aunt Céleste are always making such a big deal about things. Do you know how often I had to go to the tutors and the dean and all those guys because people complained about me? Do you know how often I wanted to hit people?'

'What did they say?' I asked.

'No, man. That's not what it's about. They also called me all kinds of shit. I just gave them as good as I got myself. You make everything far too complicated. Sometimes shit's the way it is, and that's not chill, but you shouldn't give a fuck.'

'Oh yeah,' I said, when Miriam sat down on the passenger seat with her legs outside the car. 'So none of this would have happened if I had given *less* of a fuck.'

163

She began to laugh.

There are so many books I've read in which the main character's original view of his family bites the dust. In all those books the main character always grows up at the expense of that original image.

Miriam laughing. She said: 'You're stupid, bitch.'

'You're a child. You shouldn't forget that,' Dad says now. I watch the bees on Mum's hydrangeas.

'So were they.'

'Listen,' he then says sternly, 'you're a child. Do you think I never did anything stupid when I was growing up? I was also angry. If it's anyone's fault you've turned out this way, it's mine.'

Agamemnon's father Atreus killed his brother Thyestes' sons and served up their meat at dinner. Once Thyestes had eaten his own children, Atreus got their chopped off hands and feet, which hadn't been cooked, and showed them to Thyestes. He did this because Thyestes had fucked his wife. After Agamemnon came back from Troy he was killed by his own wife, Clytemnestra. Clytemnestra in turn was killed by her son. The entire bloodline was cursed.

The structures, said Aunt Céleste, are turned against you.

What's home to you, Frits asked during one of our last sessions. What does it look like?

Since I've been back I've constantly had to pop in and out of the kitchen while I'm reading in the living room. Midway through a sentence I become aware of a buzzing or creaking in the house, as if something's on fire somewhere on the floor. Then, just as I prick up my ears, there's a temporary silence before the fridge's compressor draws power again, the humming resumes.

What's home to you, Frits asked, imagine it. Describe it.

Dad removes his hand from my neck. He leans backwards into his chair. The bees hover from the hydrangea to the lavender. The voices of laughing and screaming children ring out from the neighbourhood.

The sound of the fridge makes me nervous. The fridge that's been there for years. Since I've been home I've not been able to

164

sleep because of the birch tree's rustling, the branches that sometimes hit my open window in the wind. The barking neighbourhood
dogs making themselves heard one last time before the back doors
are locked, the curtains drawn with a tug, make me panic.

What's home? What kind of question's that?

I've tried to describe my family. Every time I did, he didn't
know what I meant.

How did I turn out this way? What should Dad and Mum have
done differently?

I tap the ash from my cigarette, which is nearly burnt down,
and I extinguish it in the pasta jar. Try to swallow the lump in my
throat.

'But it's not your fault,' I say. 'I should never have—'

'True,' says Dad, and quickly raises his hand. 'I just mean, it's
understandable.'

He stretches his arms in front of him, with the palms of his
hands against an invisible wall. He leaves his arms suspended
there, then drops them.

'Sorry that the neighbours let their dogs shit by the door the
whole time,' I say.

'When I find out who does it, they'll soon stop.'

When Paris stole his brother's wife, Agamemnon sacrificed his
own daughter in exchange for a favourable wind to get his ships
to Troy.

Miriam goes off to The Hague.

Mum does the shopping in town.

Dad smokes his cigarettes and swallows his pills with big
glasses of water.

It's just how you view things. Sacrificing your daughter.
Letting your brother eat his children. Buying a punchball for your
daughters.

When Dad takes his next cigarette from his packet and holds
it up to me, I shake my head.

'It could be the whole village, right?' I say.

Dad shrugs his shoulders while his lighter ignites.

'Doesn't interest me.'

HE DIDN'T GET WHAT I MEANT, Frits.

I began to translate the letters that Aunt Céleste had written to me over the past six months. There were three, all double-sided. She wrote that everything that'd happened was just a first step in my worldly 'awakening'.

If I couldn't get my head around the French, I went to Dad. He would then read the sentence, shake his head and roll his eyes.

'Violence is simply a first response,' Aunt Céleste wrote.

As if I can explain to Frits how it all fits together. Things just are. They've always been like that. I don't know where it all began. Whether you would call it inexplicable or not.

'Now you can focus on your true aims in life,' she wrote in another letter, 'and claim your place in the resistance against this colonial patriarchy in which you grew up. It's not your fault! You're clever and you have anger in you, that's perfectly normal. The only thing you need to do is to make it productive instead of destructive, so that you can fight for the right cause, overthrow the systems that structurally suppress you and yours.'

In her letters she wrote that she hoped I'd soon come to Barcelona. 'We can talk about these things then. The sea air will do you good.'

I no longer have nightmares now that I sleep at home. I don't dream.

What I mean is, said Frits in irritation, how come that when you're bullied your father buys you a punchball instead of asking for a meeting with your form tutor?

'I understand that it's difficult for you to understand what I'm talking about,' Aunt Céleste wrote, 'but believe me when I tell you that what you've got caught up in is about much more than bullying and juvenile revenge. Those boys represent an extremely malicious system!'

Much more than bullying and juvenile revenge. I look at Dad as he translates these words.

While I read the letters I had to think of Zainab, with her sparkling eyes, how she emptied her glass after the supervisors, two adult males, sat down on Marissa's back. Marissa herself, how she lashed out at Marco from the ground.

I've had it with those men, said Bassa as he walked away, who think this is a theme park. A theme park. A theme park with bullying and juvenile revenge. And I, who should focus on my true aims in life.

How come your mother reacts so passively, Frits asked.

How she shakes her head, oh honey oh honeybunch. That when I think of her I see her sitting at her desk, with her emails, her paperwork, whole days bent over her keyboard. How she says: 'I've no idea about that.'

I read in that Classical Studies book that, in the early days of Greek civilisation, if you'd murdered someone you had to go abroad and had to wait in the house of a stranger until the hand you committed the murder with had been washed by the man of the house, in the blood of a piglet. As a cleansing ceremony. I wonder what form that would take these days. How do you turn something destructive into something productive? Or in any case into something neutral again?

How can that be? Frits asked.

You're a child, Dad said.

What is there not to understand? I asked. What's odd about that? What do you not understand? The confusion in his eyes.

But it's not incomprehensible, is it?

Before I began to dream about that she-devil and that man, how they pull my head from my torso as we're all tumbling into the depths of the earth together, I thought I was the Fury of this shitty village, the goddess of vengeance. If that isn't the case, how should I move forward? And likewise Paul and Salvatore? Mum, Dad, Miriam, those two dudes and me?

LILIANA'S MOTHER ANSWERS THE PHONE when I ring their landline.

'Who?' she asks.

'Sa-lo-mé, Mrs Filipek,' I say. 'Is Liliana home?'

Silence. I hear Liliana's father asking something in Polish. Her mother replying.

'I couldn't find her mobile number,' I explain.

'Yes,' snaps Liliana's mother.

Liliana's parents argue while I wait. Her father raises his voice and then her mother raises her voice and then her mother says: 'Wait,' and then it's quiet until Liliana comes on the line.

'You shouldn't phone the landline, you dope,' she whispers.

'I haven't got your number,' I say.

'Damn.'

Liliana gives me her number while her father swears in the background. I think. Then she hangs up.

Ten minutes later I ring her mobile, as promised.

'Let's hang tomorrow. But don't come and get me at home,' she says, 'we'll see each other at the canal. Two p.m.?'

No one ever talks about those dudes. No one ever talks about how things got to the point that I went overboard. Why Paul's now going around with a glass eye.

A time frame. A defined period during which it's usually expected that someone who's being told about that time frame takes a particular action: accepts a package, makes an enquiry, waits for an answer from some official authority, signs up for something, submits a document, asks a violent offender: 'Why?'

There's a defined period of time, clear-cut, within which this can be done. You have a specific number of seconds, minutes, hours, days, in which to act, with the objective that afterwards, something will have changed: data has been stored, the test's been taken, the package rests in your hands, you understand how things got out of hand, understand why – exactly. Outside that defined time period it can't be done, or in any case not with the desired result.

So what's changed?

What's remained the same?

I can explain why Dad bought a punchball instead of talking to my form tutor, but there's nothing I can do about it any more. The time frame within which I can probe this has passed, has expired.

And Liliana's mother. When I phoned, before the Donut, she'd always ask how things were going at school.

You must study hard, she said. Don't be like Lili, shh, shh, she hissed jokingly through the phone.

Why did you take part in that programme?

Why didn't you visit?

Why didn't you phone?

Why did you choose me when I was already having such a fucking hard time?

I have a defined period of time. A window through which to look at the options. What can I do? A trailer has to be rented. Dad has to go to the oncologist. Prescriptions have to be collected. I need to choose a book to read. Water the plants. Mum and I have to discuss the continuation of my therapy with the social worker who deals with rehabilitation. Someone's scratched the car. Dog turds on the drive. Rubbish. Mum drove into town to do the shopping. Forgot the milk. The toilet rolls. I wipe my bum with folded sheets of kitchen towel. I lie awake hearing the birch tree's branches beating against the open window. The humming of the fridge. Miriam, who stuffs cases full of clothes into a removal box, goes to Carlita, babysits.

'Tom Joad's an ex-prisoner,' said Mum from her office chair, with her back to the bookcase, 'in *Grapes of Wrath*.'

I was looking for a book to read.

'What's it about?'

'The Great Depression.' Mum clicked her mouse and the printer sprang to life, began to rattle. 'A family loses their farm. They go to California to work. Very tragic. Beautiful.'

'And who's this Tom Joad then?'

Mum took the printouts from the printer and tapped the underside of the sheets against the desk top.

'Murder. I believe.' She didn't look at me. I looked at her.

'What?'

'He was in prison for murder. He's released at the beginning of the story. Fat book,' she said and, focussed, placed the pile of papers in the hole punch, pressed it.

'Long time since I read it.' In the file. The file back onto the shelf above the desk with the other files.

I searched on in silence. When I'd found the book I grabbed it from the shelf, read the back cover. Mum got up and went to the kitchen. I heard the tap, put the book back.

'He's the son,' I heard her say.

I need to get off this path and take another. Before the time frame has expired. I need to find out where the other Salomé is, the Salomé who's made off with all my luck, and find a way to get to her. No one ever talks about those boys. It's not all about you.

I need to put her inside me again, so that we are one, and there's balance again. Before we've passed this time frame's demarcation line. Otherwise the buzzing in my head will go on and on, like a swarm of bees. It's been doing it for a while and it should stop.

So, Miriam said.

Grab the rope. Climb out of the pit. Try to get used to the light.

Describe it. What's home to you then?

Very safe, I told Frits.

It's a beautiful day. It's an incredibly beautiful day. While Mum and Miriam are at IKEA and Dad's having his afternoon nap, I head for the canal that runs through part of the village. Cirrus clouds soften the sunlight that falls onto the emerald green grass. The water in the canal is turquoise and calm, moves glisteningly from village to town, its bank smelling of dust and algae. Shrill mechanical noises resound from the car repair workshops on the other side of the water, but not loud enough to ruin the tranquillity. Along the canal, tree branches rock back and forth on the wind. Dragonflies, bees and birds everywhere.

I stroll in a circle via the meadow behind the tennis court back to the canal bridge. On my left-hand side three horses graze in a small paddock. One comes towards me, a brown mare with a white mark on her head. She's probably hoping for something to eat. She stops in front of the fence at an angle, keeps an eye on me. The horse and I stare at each other obliquely. Her lips move comically while she snorts.

'What do you want?' I ask and she comes a step closer. I tentatively offer my hand to her and, when I notice that she doesn't react skittishly, I briefly stroke the side of her head.

'What now?' I ask. The horse snuffles my hand. 'I've got nothing on me.'

I can feel her rough, wet lips. I pat her on the head one more time and walk back to the bridge.

Each second I spend alone I become more scared that I will meet Salvatore or Paul, or worse, their parents, or worse still, parents of people I don't even know. Friends. Cousins. Brothers.

What's home to you?

Home's a place where everyone can do their thing, and I don't belong. I live on the edge and watch. I have no choice in the matter.

The women with their coiffed hair and little dogs, who stroll on the arms of their husbands to the shops. I avoid the gaze of young people, afraid that they may recognise me from school, or the paper, or just recognise me.

You're an idiot, said Marissa.

You make everything far too complicated, man, she also said.

The murderer packs his things, leaves in the depth of the night, crosses the border and runs till the sun rises over the meadows, the fields, the forest, till he reaches the first house he comes to. He takes off his cape, his sandals, forces the lock and creeps into the house. Once inside he goes over to the fire, sinks to his knees, waits until the man of the house gets out of bed.

The whole idea is of course that you subject yourself to the goodness of another person. That their mercy ensures your crime's forgiven.

What if the man of the house ignores your presence? What if you don't feel like washing your hands in the blood of a piglet?

I don't trust the man of the house. The man of the house is as sick as I am. The man of the house says: 'Cry, bitch!' The man of the house worked the entire year, became worn out. Gloop from his eye seeped through his fingers.

What I mean is, how come your father bought you a punchball instead of asking for a meeting with your tutor?

Nothing's as quiet as three bodies colliding in a meadow on the side of a B-road.

'Look at her lying there,' Salvatore laughed.

The way Marissa lashed out at Marco from the ground.

As if you're punching right through the enemy.

As if you rise up from the pit, furious. Fuck all those mother-fuckers in this motherfucking place.

A lot has happened recently.

I just have to get my diploma, I said to the new therapist, then I can go.

Do you feel safe there? he asked.

Look at me and I'll turn you into stone.

I walk home and enter the back garden through the gate. We're eating in the garden and when everyone's gone inside again I stay out there to smoke cigarettes and read until the sun goes down. Mum and Dad water the plants in the front garden, muttering to each other. Miriam's escaped to some party or other. The smell of local barbecues is still lingering in the air.

It's a fucking ominous evening and that's really just because of me.

When they get me, they'll say: You see?

You're stupid.

Look at her lying there.

When they get me, there'll be other stuff they say.

Luckily I live at the edge. If I wait long enough, the time frame will have passed, the opportunity to get gone. Forgotten. No longer makes any difference. Maybe they don't want to anyway.

In Greek tragedies someone always dies at the end.

You won't find any answers in those books, you know, Dad says when he sees me reading in the garden.

The past few days I've been walking past the local supermarket and buying a sandwich and eating it wearily. I went into the church, but didn't dare go to confession. I watched the old people who moved, hunched over, towards Maria with Jesus on her arm, and left. I walked to the asylum seekers' centre, gazed outside the fence at the buildings, which, with their small windows, looked like Miriam's removal boxes, stacked on the lawn. No one going inside or coming out. No man with a cloud coat. The little school has been taken down. The children are now mixed in with the village children at the Catholic primary school.

Rehabilitate. Returning to an earlier state. Being cleansed of the taint I'm tainted with. I don't want to return to an earlier state. This isn't what I'm going to do.

What I'm going to do is not walk towards the village, but in a different direction, via the apple orchard at the edge of our neighbourhood towards the street leading out of the village, towards the farms along a big, wide road that people barely drive on at this hour of the day.

Tonight a warm wind's blowing and the wind pushes me forwards, towards the fields. When I look up I see a crescent moon, some stars, especially now that I'm leaving the village with its lamp posts. When the road becomes a track it's really dark; this is where the lamp posts stop. As I walk past the fields, I hear people whoop drunkenly in the distance.

The houses get bigger, have had extensions built. Their yards become fields. Swimming pool filters whir in the water. Trampolines and go-karts and cars glisten in the silver moonlight. And then more meadows, fields, nothing, until you get to the next farm. The odd sign: BIEMANS. ROOIJAKKER. VAN DRUNEN. RAAIJMAKERS BEAUTY SALON. MEEUWIS. CUCUMBER FARM VAN DE ZANDT.

The blood of a piglet.

I'm at the edge. I'm in between everything. I get it. I totally get it. I follow the track, along the maize fields, cabbage, lettuce, strawberries and grass. The barbed wire, the ditches along the sides of the path, the horse shit I narrowly avoid. Then I finally see the small, faint spotlights that illuminate the grounds of his house. I stop in front of the drive, jump over the ditch that separates the track from the property, creep into the yard.

This is where I need to be, to see it.

Here are your hands, your feet.

Here's the child that you sacrificed for a favourable wind.

They've given that dude a glass eye, said Miriam. By the way.

Frits said in one of our sessions, before he went on holiday, that it's important I connect. How, I asked him, should I connect if everything around me is so dismal?

I wriggle on my haunches over the grass. In my head I've done this hundreds of times. I don't know if they have a dog, but it'll be asleep inside, if it's there at all. The house stands between two conifer hedges, neatly trimmed, behind that I hear voices, see the sparks of a fire flickering over the top of the hedges.

But it's not at all dismal, he said, you're clever, you can go and do a degree.

You're clever. You're stupid. I'm *not* a racist.

At least there's no light in front of the veranda, no sensor. I can hear them, but they're sitting behind the house, protected by the hedges and the enormous garage. They've had a barbecue or something, mellow with the children. I'm sure they don't know that I'm back. That I've crept into the village like a coward, without big announcements, without fanfare, neither my mug nor my name in the paper.

Inside there's light on and I move on my hands and knees through the grass. I have to see it. Their accents are so broad I can hardly understand them. Beer bottles click, but it's at the rear, behind the house.

I crawl over the lawn towards the windowsill and sit down underneath it. I hear the TV and I watch; I have to get used to the light, but I watch. I watch.

The TV, *X Factor* or something like that, and the brown leather sofa. The typical interior of the street's old-fashioned farms: massive wooden sideboards and glass display cases for Swarovski crystal, the family portraits above the enormous TV. No one's sitting on the sofas or chairs. The living room's empty. The dog's lying asleep in his basket and there are dishes on the dining table.

From behind the house loud laughter rings out. I take a deep breath and crawl left along the hedge, around the house, the garden. If I stay low I may be able to see it.

If you could go back, would you have done it differently? I can no longer go back, I say to Frits.

You're a child, said Dad.

By the way.

It could be the entire village, right, but the entire village doesn't interest me. It's this dude, the cyclops who doesn't even know how to pronounce my name.

They're sitting on a paved patio. A brazier, four comfy garden chairs, a table full of food and beer. I see a mother wrapped in a shawl, with blonde hair, a father clad in a checked shirt, a young woman with her hair in a tall bun. It could be the entire village.

It's not me anyway.

And the boy with the glass eye. I see Paul. He's sitting and he's drinking. He doesn't look up. No one sees me. He doesn't know that I'm staring at him from afar while he's drinking in his garden. When I gaze long enough I see how the light from the brazier reflects differently in one eye from the other, as if one's been polished and the other hasn't. He stares ahead. There's more laughter, but he doesn't join in. He drinks.

I visualise how I hit him. How the bit sticking out from a snapped twig must have penetrated into his eye socket, how he wailed, I can't even remember if he wailed, and how he began to scream and then bleat hysterically and rolled and rolled and was completely indifferent to the cowpat he landed in with his North Face coat and excessively expensive Nikes. And he takes another swig with his thin, chapped lips, his fuzzy tache and spotty upper lip, his blond curls like a sheep, and gnawed nails, his broken middle and ring finger, in plaster, his shirt too big around his puny shoulders, the shite in his hair, how he rolls and rolls and rolls, his socks pulled up too high and his oversized shorts. I know exactly what he looks like, even though he's sitting a long way from me. I don't see the difference between one eye and the other. He will always view things differently. I know that now, even if I don't see it.

The evening wind's blowing and their talking sounds like buzzing. My hands on the earth, on my knees, my head angled in such a way that I can look through the hedge. He's a lonely chicken in the coop and I'm the fox.

You wait for the man of the house for the cleansing ritual.

That's required. That's what should be done.

He takes another swig. I see him laugh, on his bike with Salvatore next to him, and the noises they make, but it's too boring.

I'm mimicking you.

With your mumbo jumbo.

That grin. And after those panicky tears, covered in shite, blood streaming down his cheeks, his eye gloop seeping through his fingers as he lies splayed out on the ground. I'm still holding on to the stick. He convulses, is shaking all over. In shock. I'm still holding on to the stick as Salvatore wraps his arms around my head, starts to pull me away from him by my head, pressing the inside of his elbows against my neck.

I'd forgotten it, but it's back. Hyperventilating and wailing, oh my eye, what the fuck, my eye. Like a child. His groaning and terrified primordial behaviour that you'd expect from a wounded dog. I don't know.

I'll kill you, is what Salvatore screamed. I'll kill that bitch. How I hit him with the stick raised over my head.

It's no longer about what I should or shouldn't have done and whether it was right or not. It's no longer about whether some goal or other was achieved. It's not about the barbed wire, how my chin got caught in it when I climbed underneath it.

I must simply see it.

I punished them. The coins on the ground and how the man in the cloud coat walked away. He needs money, doesn't he?

I'm mimicking you.

Walked away from his flailing body.

I'll kill that bitch, is what Salvatore screamed. Both of us hanging over him as he was lying there and Salvatore screaming and me looking on, and him screaming and grabbing my head and pulling and me over my head and both of us falling on top of him and turning around and me pummelling. How he lay there without moving. Salvatore curled up.

Don't touch me, he called, fucking animal, don't touch me.

Turned around and walked away.

Everyone's safe, Miriam said, and everything's okay.

I slowly crawl backwards, until I'm far enough away from the hedge to stand up. A moped scoots past somewhere. The moped passes me and doesn't stop. I want Miriam. I want my sister. I want my Dad and my Mum at the edge of the village.

I hate men who think this is a fucking theme park.

I was lying. I didn't see a nonentity when I saw Frits sitting in his chair. I didn't see a stupid, sad old man. I still saw that creep with his hands on the girl's back. Dad going across the garden with his rake. Miriam being grabbed by the throat. Me jumping into the tree. Us driving through shanty towns and Miriam gazing at the corrugated iron roofs with her face pressed against the window. The aunt with her low voice. She looks like you. You're a child. You are better than this.

The structures are turned against you. It's important that you learn to deal with that.

How do you turn something destructive into something productive?

What I'm trying to say is that I get it. I really get it. A farmer falls asleep in the shadow of a tree one spring afternoon, next to his flock of grazing sheep. When he wakes up his sheep are still there, his dogs and his horse. The mare's still tied to the tree. His gun's lying there as well. But the farmer's shaken up. As if, in his sleep, he stepped through something, jumped through something, not of his own free will, unawares.

During his trek back, the sheep are restless, the dogs are doing their best, but they're tired, as if their bodies are moving through sand instead of grass. The farmer has cotton wool in his brain, leans over his horse's back as if he's drunk. His body feels too big for the movements he wants to make. It seems to expect something very strange from him, is restless and is fighting against something, but he doesn't know what. He begins to check out what makes him himself. He still has a mole in the dimple of his left collar bone, he knows his name, the day, that flowers will bloom shortly and that he'll be able to sleep without the woollen bedspread. He knows that this path will end in a fork and that he'll go left and that that way he'll be home the quickest. And he goes home like a child in the fog, as if the dusty, sandy path will disappear under his feet, but it doesn't. The daily routine of looking after his flock, his dogs, his horse, he carries out those things as if it's an ancient dance. It strikes him as so strange. How did it come to this? The farmer sees all the familiar elements of his life around him and yet something's changed. All of a sudden it all seems so different from what he thought. The trees are different, the mountain in the distance peaks peculiarly towards the evening sky, and once home, the horse stabled again, his gun in its rightful place, his coat and shoes off, he is overcome by the most intense terror. You didn't see what you thought you were seeing. As if, despite the fact that everything's still in the world in the same way as before, he's stepped from a blurred photo into the clear truth of his life.

I get it, didn't I say? Medusa's head is chopped off. Sula's death was celebrated by the villagers. Spirits spit on Léonie van Oudijck in the bath. Ophelia commits suicide. Emma Bovary drinks arsenic, I couldn't get through the book, but I looked it up. Maya has another baby. The farmer wakes up from his dream.

My breath wheezes out of my lungs. I don't know.

I pace back and forth over Paul's family's lawn.

A pick-up full of screeching women roars past. They're drinking beer on the loading platform, the typical jumpstyle bass drones thumping into the night and they fling their empty bottles out of the pick-up onto the ground.

Now you can focus on your true aims in life.

I'm thirsty. I stink of sweat from all the walking and hauling today. I'm parched. How do you turn something destructive into something productive? I've done my time. I don't know.

My name is Salomé Atabong, I want to tell Paul. Not bloody monkey or fucking animal or fucking nigger. You have to say it properly: Salomé Henriette Constance Atabong. I stop pacing back and forth and feel the cold over my entire body; it draws up from the ground into my body. I look at my body, my hands, feet, my legs and torso and then upwards. Clear, the stars. When I stretch my palms to the sky, I push right through them, that's how big I am. I'm so fucking big.

Salomé Henriette Constance Atabong. I want to hear you say it. I want you to shout it at me.

I run to the hedge, close my eyes and jump through the conifers. The branches hit me in the face. The four people drinking beer in the back garden look up startled. I stand in the garden with all my atoms. I'm not on the edge, I'm bang in the middle. If time doesn't start ticking differently of its own accord then I'll trash the clock with my own two hands.

'Here I am,' I call with my arms in the air, I'm shaking all over, it feels light. 'Here I am.'

My fingerprints are stored in a centre. My atoms are all here. The dog barks inside. The father jumps up. Paul with his glass eye and open mouth slams the beer bottle on the table.

'My name is Salomé,' I say, 'Salomé Henriette Constance Atabong. That's me.'

Acknowledgements

While writing this book I have used the following sources:

Netherlands Custodial Institutions Act (*Beginselenwet justitiële inrichtingen*), https://wetten.overheid. nl/bwbr0011756/2020-01-01.
Kraak, Marijn, *Groeten uit de Rimboe? Een onderzoek naar de reality soaps Groeten uit de Rimboe en Groeten Terug (Greetings from the Jungle? A Study into the Reality Soaps Greetings from the Jungle and All the Best to You Too),* (Uitgeverij Aksant, 2010).

I have also conducted some interviews to guide me with the descriptions of daily life in a juvenile detention centre. Thank you Mohammed, Malcolm and, of course, Elizabeth Vrieling of Young in Prison for your crucial help and candour.

The Donut is a fictional institution. Its rules and hierarchy are based on reality but do not directly reflect it.

I would also like to thank the Lebowski team, notably Jasper Henderson; Oscar van Gelderen; Lisette Verhagen at PFD; Leonora Craig Cohen at Serpent's Tail; my translator Suzanne Heukensfeldt Jansen, and of course my beloved family.